"Are you going back to San Antonio?"

"I don't know," she said. "I resigned my commission. There's nothing there now except the past. There are friends, of course, but their lives revolve around the air force." She stopped. "I don't know why I'm babbling about this." Her gaze met his. Electricity ran between them, sparking and sizzling in ways that baffled her. She swallowed hard, then tried to break the spell. "I'm not used to being aimless," she admitted.

"I understand that," he said. "Do you feel comfortable riding outside a ring?"

"I think it depends on the horse," she said cautiously.

"I can find one. It'll be an hour before Julie finishes the lesson and cools down the horse. There are two more parents arriving, but they shouldn't be here before noon." He paused, then added, "Would you like to see more of the ranch on horseback?"

Don't go, a voice inside warned her.

Instead, she nodded and hoped she wouldn't make a fool out of herself.

Dear Reader,

I've always been intrigued by mustangs. My first effort in writing was a story about wild horses when I was eight.

In *Colorado Rancher*, I can revisit the subject along with writing what I like writing best—a romance between two people whose differences are so profound it's difficult to see how they can ever get together, but then they find a way to do exactly that.

In this case, there couldn't be two more different people than rancher Reese Howard and fighter pilot Lauren MacInnes. One loves the land. The other loves the sky.

Reese Howard's ranch has been in the family since the 1800s. His passion is saving wild mustangs and helping youngsters who've lost a military parent. Air Force Major MacInnes's daughter is badly injured in an accident that killed Lauren's husband. All she wants is to help her daughter heal.

Fortunately, Reese and Lauren wrote their own ending.

But I'll give you a hint. It's through a combination of kids, dogs, horses, a storm and an uncooperative computer that they learn love makes anything possible.

Happy reading!

Pat

HOME *on the* RANCH

COLORADO RANCHER

PATRICIA POTTER

♦ HARLEQUIN® HOME ON THE RANCH

Recycling programs
for this product may
not exist in your area.

ISBN-13: 978-1-335-54301-1
ISBN-13: 978-1-335-63400-9 (Direct to Consumer edition)

Home on the Ranch: Colorado Rancher

Copyright © 2019 by Patricia Potter

Printed in U.S.A.

USA TODAY bestselling author **Patricia Potter** always knew writing was her future, but storytelling was diverted when curiosity steered her into journalism.

Storytelling, though, won out, and she has since written more than seventy books and novellas, ranging from historical to suspense to contemporary romance.

She has received numerous writing awards, including the *RT Book Reviews* Storyteller of the Year Award, the Career Achievement Award for Western Historical Romance and Best Hero of the Year. She is a seven-time RITA® Award finalist and a three-time Maggie Award winner.

She is a past president of the Georgia Romance Writers, River City Romance Writers and Romance Writers of America.

Books by Patricia Potter

Home on the Ranch: Colorado Cowboy

Harlequin Superromance

Home to Covenant Falls

The Soldier's Promise
Tempted by the Soldier
A Soldier's Journey
The SEAL's Return

Visit the Author Profile page
at Harlequin.com for more titles.

Dedicated to the many ranchers and farmers who offer Horses for Heroes programs for troubled veterans and for the families of fallen soldiers.

Prologue

Bagram Air Force Base, Afghanistan

The SEAL team was in trouble.

Her adrenaline running high, Air Force Major Lauren MacInnes turned her Eagle II fighter toward a mountainous area of Afghanistan. She'd been alerted to assist, if necessary, a team of SEALs sent to capture a top Taliban leader.

As she flew at a low altitude, Oscar, her weapons system operator in the backseat, located the SEAL team and concentrated on the images of figures converging on them. The SEALs had been notified of unwelcome company and were taking defensive positions.

She held steady on the course as Oscar monitored the information coming from the drone and the Eagle's sensor equipment, and then fired on the oncoming enemy.

She watched as the ground below erupted into flashes

of light. She stayed in the sky, flying at a low altitude, until the SEALs signaled "Thanks, mission accomplished." Then she and Oscar exchanged banter on the way back to base.

She was exhilarated. It was one of the good days. The SEALs had captured their objective with no casualties on their side. That high was what kept her in the air force. It held the same attraction for her husband.

Lauren took fierce pride in being one of the few women fighter pilots, but she feared it would come to an end soon. Her daughter needed a mother at home.

Lauren landed. Her stomach clenched when she saw two corporals waiting for her as she left the plane. "The colonel is waiting for you," one said as if Lauren had purposely delayed her return.

It had to be important. In the years she'd been deployed, she'd never had such a curt summons. She was not only met, but also escorted. She grew even more concerned when they headed directly toward her commanding officer's office, bypassing the adjutant. One of the corporals knocked on the door and received a short "Come in," in response.

Lauren took a deep breath. Her superior's response meant Colonel Adams had cleared his calendar for this encounter. Several possible scenarios ran through her mind. Had she not finished the job? Had they accidentally hit one or more SEALs? Or the village?

She was particularly alarmed when the colonel stood when she entered. She saluted and waited for the dressing-down she feared was coming.

"Sit down," the colonel said, motioning to a chair in front of her. He turned to the escorts. "Dismissed."

When Lauren sat straight up in the uncomfortable

chair, Colonel Adams sat down on the corner of his crowded desk. "I have bad news, Lauren."

Lauren sat up even straighter. She was eager to end this deployment and get home to her husband and daughter, but not the wrong way.

"It's your husband, Lauren," Adams said slowly. "There's no easy way to say this. Dane was killed last night in an automobile accident. Your daughter was injured. You're needed back home. As of now you're on compassionate leave."

Lauren stopped breathing. She felt as though she'd been slugged in her sternum. She'd misheard, surely. It didn't make sense. Dane was back in the States. He should be safe. Both he and her daughter. He was a damned good driver as well as a pilot, especially when Julie was with him.

"No," she said. "It must be a mistake. He's a great driver."

"It was a drunk driver. He T-boned them on the driver's side. I'm sorry, Lauren."

It was a nightmare. Not real. She couldn't accept the fact Dane was gone. She clenched her fists and willed herself to breathe. *Concentrate.* "Julie was injured? How badly?"

"From what I understand, she has serious but not critical injuries." He handed Lauren a sheet of paper. "Here are contacts for you. The hospital, the chaplain, Julie's doctors. I have you on a military flight to Germany in two hours and another to the States an hour after you arrive in Germany."

Lauren was still too stunned to say anything, to feel the pain she knew was coming. Dane was so damn competent at everything he did. A drunk driver, her colonel had said. He simply couldn't die that way.

A windstorm of loss swept over her. She and Dane met in pilot training. They were rivals, then friends and finally lovers. When they discovered the new Joint Spouse Program would allow them to stay together, it was just the excuse they needed to exchange rings. Their daughter, Julie, was born two years later in Germany.

He'd recently been promoted and transferred to San Antonio where she thought he would be safe.

Lauren closed her eyes and prayed Julie wasn't hurt badly. She couldn't think about Dane. Not now. She curled her fingers around the paper to avoid shouting out in denial. Instead, she tried to prioritize. She couldn't do anything for Dane now. *Concentrate on Julie.*

"Everything I know is contained on that paper," Colonel Adams said after giving her a moment to absorb the news. "Hospital and physician numbers. You should be able to reach the hospital for a progress report and they're waiting on you to contact them. They can't do anything but emergency medicine without your approval."

He paused, then added, "Major Marsh and his wife are staying at the hospital with your daughter until you arrive, and you have his number. I understand you are close friends."

Too numb to speak, she just nodded.

He paused. "I'm so sorry, Lauren. It's damned unfair. If there's anything I can do, just name it."

Lauren rose from the chair. She would have to rush to get everything together in an hour. "Thanks for arranging everything," she managed to say.

"I would hate to lose you," Colonel Adams said.

"You're one of my best pilots and you did a damn good job today. There are eight SEALs still alive because of you." He hesitated, then added, "Dane was a damned fine pilot and a good guy."

Was.

Instead of *is*. The realization was a body blow.

Numb, she walked to her quarters and changed from her flying uniform into civilian clothes. She packed her duffel. The last item was the photo of Dane and Julie together.

Chapter 1

Fifteen Months Later
Colorado

A miracle. Just a small one. Or maybe a big one. Just this once...

"We're running ahead of schedule." Bob Marsh, long-time friend and fellow pilot, interrupted Lauren Mac-Innes's silent prayer.

Early is good. They were on a tight timetable. Lauren's fingers twisted together as she looked out the window of the four-seat Beechcraft that Bob and three of his air force friends owned. It was good to be in the air again but she ached to be at the controls of the plane. It had been a month since she piloted one.

But it was Bob's plane, and she'd made a promise to her daughter that she wouldn't fly again. She hadn't said anything about not being a passenger.

"Tell me more about this program," Bob said. "This was rather sudden, wasn't it?"

"It's a month-long equine therapy program for kids of fallen soldiers, especially those with physical or emotional problems," she replied. "Patti suggested it several weeks ago. Problem was the slots were filled, then two days ago someone dropped out and there was an opening. It begins in three weeks. I wanted to check it out before mentioning it to Julie."

"How did Patti learn about it? By the way, my wife thinks she's terrific."

"So do I. Patti's part of the family now. I don't know what I'll do when she goes back to graduate school. She's been a godsend since I found her through our doctor."

Lauren thought about the months Patti had worked for them. Lauren had hired her as a temporary caregiver for Julie after her daughter's second surgery. It had worked so well, she'd stayed for the next nine months while Lauren finished her military commitment. Patti was a student in physical therapy and was taking as many online courses as possible before returning to the campus.

"I thought I was getting someone temporarily to stay with Julie—instead, I found a friend who's great with her." She sighed. "But to answer your question, she's related to the ranch owner in some extended way—like a second cousin once removed or something—and worked at the ranch after high school graduation. It's one reason she's studying physical therapy.

"Time," Lauren added, "is crucial, which is why I shanghaied you. I can't send Julie someplace I've never seen." She hesitated, then added, "Something has to bring Julie out of her depression. I haven't been able to do it. She was so close to Dane. Worst thing is she still blames herself for his death."

"It was a drunk driver," Bob said.

"I know that, and you know that, but she believes that if she hadn't asked Dane to stop for ice cream after winning that regional meet, they wouldn't have been on that road. Therapy hasn't helped much. Neither has the fact that she doesn't know if she will ever walk normally again."

"The poor kid sure has had it rough," he said. "So have you. I wish there was more Sue and I could have done."

"You two were there when we needed you," Lauren replied. "As well as now."

"How much do you know about this program?"

"Not as much as I would like to know," she said. "I consulted with Julie's orthopedist and the psychologist at the military hospital. The psychologist was already familiar with equine therapy and checked out this program. All the feedback was positive. I did what research I could find on equine therapy in the past few days, but I need more information."

"What does Julie think about it?"

"I haven't mentioned it to her yet. The ranch uses wild mustangs in the program, and I'm not too sure about that. Couldn't that be dangerous? And how would she mount a horse with that brace?"

He didn't reply for a moment, then asked, "Any movement with the foot yet?"

"No, but the doctor said it could take weeks before we know whether the last operation was successful."

"Well, if anyone can make it happen, it's Julie," Bob replied.

"The old Julie could. I'm not sure about this one. She's so discouraged, it breaks my heart. She sits there for hours just willing that darn toe to move and there's no movement."

He nodded. He and his wife, Sue, had been at the hospital the night of the accident and stayed by Julie's side until Lauren arrived. They had been with Lauren during subsequent operations.

"It's so damn frustrating, Bob," Lauren said. "She has to teach a muscle to do what the nerve did. Her orthopedist told her to concentrate on moving the toes and warned that some patients never learn to do it. If it is successful, she'll have some control over the ankle and foot. Otherwise, the foot will just drop. It would be an impediment. Amputation could be the next step."

"Wow," he said. "I didn't know it was that tough."

Lauren shrugged. "I know how busy you are with this new promotion. Sue's been terrific, and I love her for it. She's always bringing books and small gifts to Julie, and I can't thank you enough for ferrying me here today." She paused, then confessed, "I'm not even sure whether I really want her to do this program. I don't want her to fail. Or, God forbid, get injured again." Her voice broke and she hated that. She didn't cry. Warriors didn't cry.

Except she wasn't a warrior any longer. Nor a very good mom. She just couldn't reach her daughter. She'd almost given up on miracles when Patti suggested they try equine therapy for Julie.

It seemed far-fetched in the beginning. Julie might be able to walk but only with crutches and a brace. How could she ride a horse? Then Lauren went online and researched equine therapy. There did seem to be miracles.

But mustangs?

That part of it worried her. Something, however, had to change. The fifteen months since the accident had been a continuous nightmare. The worst had been telling her daughter her father was dead. Then she had to tell Julie that her leg had been crushed. It was a question of whether they could save it. It still was.

It hadn't helped that Lauren had a dangerous occupation, one that ended a month ago when she'd completed her current service commitment. After her compassionate and accrued leave ended, she'd been transferred to Lackland Air Force Base near San Antonio where she was an instructor.

When she'd fulfilled her commitment, she resigned.

She really had no choice. Other than burying her husband, leaving the air force was the hardest thing she'd ever done. She'd spent most of her life dreaming of being an air force pilot, working to be a pilot, then being a pilot. But Julie had to come first. Her daughter had been terrified she would lose her mother as well as her dad and begged Lauren not to re-up. There was no other family. No siblings, or grandparents. No one. It was just the two of them now.

As if reading her mind, Bob glanced over at her. "It's been hell for you, hasn't it?"

"Worse for Julie," she said. "She adored Dane. I'm an adult. I've learned to survive loss. She's only fifteen and she's had to deal with losing her father and the guilt that she somehow is responsible for it. She's also lost her lodestone, the challenge that drove her so hard." Her daughter had been an athlete who dreamed of competing in the Olympics, and her injuries were devastating to who and what she'd been.

Bob nodded. He'd been to some of the track competitions in Texas while Lauren was in Germany. Julie won each one. Lauren knew Julie had inspired his own children to compete.

"I'm hoping, no, make that praying, this program could help her heal emotionally," Lauren said. "She's always loved animals, and Dane and I never felt we could have one since we never knew where we would be assigned next."

"We're approaching the descent," Bob announced. "It sure looks like scenic country down there."

"Patti showed me some photos. It's breathtaking. The Eagles' Roost Ranch is one of the few large family-owned ranches left in Colorado."

"Eagles' Roost? I like the name."

"I do, too," she said. She recalled every word Patti had said when she first recommended it after Julie had a particularly bad day.

"Know anything about this family?" he asked.

"There's apparently just the owner, his sister and her son. Patti warned me that sometimes the owner comes across as impatient, or even rude. In addition to running the ranch, he teaches horsemanship and even makes videos used as teaching tools. Comes by the talent honestly, according to Patti, since he's one fourth Ute. They were considered among the best horsemen of the western tribes."

"Sounds interesting anyway," Bob said.

"And too good," Lauren said darkly. She'd gotten the opinion that her employee and friend had ulterior purposes, like playing cupid.

Bob chuckled. "Anything else?"

"According to her, the ranch has been in his family since Colorado was settled. His father had a bad accident when he was twenty and in his second year at the University of Colorado School of Agriculture. He dropped out and has been running the ranch since."

She omitted the rest of Patti's description: *He's the tall, silent type. Sometimes Reese comes across as curt, but he's a really nice guy once you get to know him.*

"Any reason he's offering this program?" Bob asked.

"I asked the same thing. According to Patti, he's passionate about saving wild mustangs, especially after he learned they usually respond well to emotionally and physically wounded children and vice versa. He started exploring possibilities. This is the fourth year he's sponsored programs for them."

"Sounds like an interesting guy," Bob said. "Married?"

She shrugged. When a year passed since Dane's death, Bob and Sue tried to get her to mix more with fellow pilots. She wasn't interested. Julie was all that mattered now. Not only that, this Reese Howard probably had a wife and six kids. She hadn't asked, and Patti hadn't offered more information.

She looked down at the scenery below. The plains had been replaced by the foothills. The roads below were winding, and the structures farther and farther apart as they approached the local airstrip.

Bob glanced at his watch. "The wind's been with us," he said. "We're going to be there early." They'd left San Antonio at 7:00 a.m. and they'd guessed their arrival would be around eleven-thirty for the noon meeting.

Her plan was to stay no more than three hours, hopefully more like two. That would get them back home before dark.

After a smooth landing, Bob parked the plane and

went to make arrangements to refuel it for their return to San Antonio that afternoon. She walked to the small, nearly empty building to check on a rental car she'd ordered yesterday. The one person at the desk inside the small building told her it had arrived and gave her the keys and paperwork.

She checked her watch. They were on time. Sally Reynolds, sister of the owner, had offered to pick them up, but Lauren preferred the independence of renting a car since she wasn't sure when they would land. She hadn't been sure she could rent one here but obviously if you paid enough, you could rent anything, anytime, anywhere.

This "anything" was an elderly Jeep, but it was clean inside and when she started it, it ran well.

As she waited for Bob, she glanced at the information she'd acquired about the Eagles' Roost Ranch and its equine therapy program, Junior Ranchers. She'd made a list of questions she wanted to ask and started to review them.

The military had taught her to be prepared and be on time; two rules she tried never to break.

Reese Howard swore as he looked ahead at the line of traffic. He was late. He hated being late for anything. It had been ingrained in him as a child. You don't keep people waiting on you.

Especially if they were coming six hundred or more miles.

An accident on the main highway from the mustang sale in Wyoming had slowed traffic to a crawl. For the past three hours he'd followed a long line of cars, trucks and even a bus or two over an alternate route. After leaving the main flow he still had to drive fifty miles over a winding two lane road. Not fun when he was hauling four terrified horses and a cantankerous, and vocal, burro for seven hours.

Problems started at the mustang auction in Wyoming. He'd gone to buy four new mustangs for the program that had become so important to him. One for each of the incoming kids. The sale had dragged on, and he'd had a confrontation with another bidder over a black mare. He won that battle and paid far more than the usual one hundred and twenty-five dollars per mustang just off the range, but he'd liked her spirit. It was obvious from her eyes she was frightened, but she still stood defiant.

He'd already selected three other mares, but he really wanted the black one. Properly bred, she could produce some great colts and fillies.

And the burro? No one wanted him. The Bureau of Land Management wanted to get rid of him. Now he was kicking up a storm in his horse trailer and further frightening the mustangs, if that was possible.

He'd purchased the lot for nine hundred dollars. The burro was thrown in free. Reese still wasn't quite sure why he accepted the offer. Burros always created chaos, but this one looked so damn forlorn as he stood isolated among his larger relatives. Darn if he hadn't reminded Reese of a burro he'd had as a kid.

He was eager to return to Eagles' Roost. The mustangs weren't used to being confined in a small space and were nervous. No. *Petrified* was the right word. In the past few days, they'd been driven from public range into pens by helicopters, then separated from the herd that had protected them since they were born.

The plan was to train and sell them to good homes

at top prices while helping veterans and their kids at the same time. It also meant four less mustangs would starve in hostile environments or be sold and resold to questionable buyers.

He looked ahead at the blocked road again, tried his cell again—still no service—and uttered a few more choice words.

Chapter 2

"Quite a place!" Bob Marsh echoed Lauren's thoughts as she drove through the open five-bar gate. A sign overhead announced their destination: Eagles' Roost Ranch.

"It's a lot larger than I expected," he added. "It seems to go on forever."

The ranch was in a valley shadowed on one side by a large jagged mountain. For the last mile, the land beside the road was lined with a thick wire fence. Horses grazed in several paddocks, and cattle were visible in the distance.

She reduced speed as she drove down the gravel road toward a cluster of buildings dominated by a large rambling white house with a wraparound porch. What looked like stables were located on both sides of the house, each with its own riding ring and paddock. She saw parts of other buildings behind the stables.

Lauren had just parked when a woman burst through

the front door of the house with all the energy of a tornado and walked over to the Jeep as she was stepping out.

"Mrs. MacInnes?" the woman said, then answered her own question. "But of course you are. Patti described you perfectly. I'm Sally Reynolds. We talked on the phone. I understand you don't have much time, so we'll get started. Reese is running late, so I'll fill you in until he arrives."

Sally was tall and athletically built. She looked to be in her midthirties. She wore jeans, boots, a leather jacket and an easy smile. Her glance went to Bob.

"This is Major Marsh," Lauren said. "He flew me down here."

"Welcome to Eagles' Roost, Major," Sally said.

"Make it Bob," he said.

"I understand you flew from San Antonio. How was the flight?"

"Great," Bob said. "Clear skies. The landscape was spectacular flying in. Mountains. Lakes. Forest. Even saw a herd of antelope."

"This is really the best time of the year," Sally said. "Winter is also breathtaking but it gets darn cold."

"I didn't realize there were ranches up here," Bob said.

"We're a disappearing breed," Sally replied. "Most of the cleared land is being sold for residential and recreational uses. The few existing ranches in the area are mostly family owned and have been operating for a century or more." She changed the subject. "Have you had anything to eat?"

"A huge jug of coffee and day-old pastries," Bob admitted.

"Then have some lunch. There's stew simmering on the stove…and bread just out of the oven."

"That sounds great," Lauren broke in, "but we're really on a tight schedule."

"Reese should be here shortly. He's on the road back from buying some mustangs for the program. Something must have delayed him, and cell service out here is iffy at best. In the meantime, we can talk about the ranch and the program while you eat something. Reese should be here by the time we finish."

Disappointment flooded her. She'd received the impression from Patti that the entire program here was his idea, as was the use of mustangs. She'd read a lot about equine therapy in the past week. It was obviously a growing field, but this was one of the few in which wild mustangs were woven into it. That was the part of the program she wanted to discuss. She wanted to be reassured about safety.

Until the accident, Julie had boundless curiosity and didn't understand the meaning of danger. Lauren didn't want that sometimes reckless curiosity to return in the midst of wild horses. On the other hand, the mention of mustangs might well be the lure to bring her to Eagles' Roost.

Despite her irritation, Lauren had no choice but to wait for Mr. Howard. Bob had taken one of his few off days to fly her up here and she couldn't ask him to do it again. She could have borrowed the plane and flown herself but she had to think about Julie now. It was simply safer with two experienced pilots on the plane.

"I'm glad you wanted to visit before sending your daughter here," Sally said, ushering them up the front steps and into the large ranch house. "In fact, it's usually mandatory for both parent and child. But since Patti had personal knowledge and thought your daughter would be a good fit for us, we waived it. But you know best about what your daughter needs."

"Not any longer," Lauren replied wryly, "unless you can turn the clock back fifteen months. She's changed from the hard-charging athlete, but maybe even then I didn't know her as well as I thought I did."

"I wonder whether we ever do," Sally said. "I'm learning new things about my son every day. Now, what about that stew? Betty Baker, our cook, is terrific."

Lauren smiled at the name.

"I know," Sally said. "But the name surely fits. She's a great cook."

Lauren was hungry and knew Bob must be, as well. "Sounds good," she said. She would have to curb her impatience to meet Reese Howard.

"Great. Patti has told me about your daughter but I would like to hear the story from you," Sally said as she led the way inside a large kitchen with two large stoves and numerous pans hanging everywhere. A pot, exuding delicious smells, was on the stove. Sally ladled stew into three large bowls and put them on a small table to the side of the kitchen. She added hot bread from the oven. "Iced tea or lemonade?" she asked.

Lauren hadn't had lemonade in years. "Lemonade," both she and Bob said together.

The aroma from the stew had not lied. It was terrific: thick with tender meat and potatoes, corn, onions and mushrooms with a tangy base. "Nearly everything comes from the ranch," Sally said as she joined them at the table. "Now, tell me about Julie."

Lauren took a deep breath. The details of that day

were still so vivid. "We—my husband and I—were stationed in Germany with alternating deployments to Afghanistan. One of us was always in Germany with Julie.

"Julie flourished there. She loved athletics and excelled at track. She won most of the track competitions in which she was eligible. She liked other sports as well, but it was track she loved. We traveled all over Europe when we were on leave. Nineteen months ago Dane was promoted and transferred to Laughlin Military Base in Texas. There were fighter pilot shortages because of the war in Afghanistan, and I couldn't get an immediate transfer.

"We gave Julie a choice," she continued. "She chose the States. She was thirteen, nearly fourteen then, and hadn't lived here since she was seven. Dane wanted her to know her own country, and Julie wanted to train in the States. To be honest, she was a daddy's girl. He adored her. I was always the disciplinarian. And then, too, she had her heart set on the Olympics, and America seemed to be the best place for her to train."

"That's a big goal."

"Julie had big dreams but they weren't completely out of the question. She flew on the track and worked at it endlessly."

Sally nodded. "Patti told me about the accident and her injuries."

"She won't run in the Olympics," Lauren said flatly. "She'll be lucky to run at all. But I'm hoping there are other sports that might interest her. Like riding. She does love animals. It's one reason I thought she might like this program."

"How's the leg now?"

"More hopeful. She's had four operations. The leg was

torn up. They had to reset it twice. The first time it didn't work. The second time they transplanted bone from her hip into her leg. Nerves and ligaments were torn in her ankle and she couldn't move her foot. They took some muscle from her ankle and substituted it for a nerve so she can have some movement there. That's where we are now. Waiting to see if it works. Even if it does, the movement will never be as it once was, but she won't have a drop foot."

Lauren hesitated, then continued. "The question is, then, how can she ride? It would break her heart to sit back and watch others."

"You don't have to worry about that. Not with all the precautions Reese takes," Sally said. "He has equipment to help riders with disabilities mount, and he also has a horse that's been trained to lie down while someone mounts. I'm a trained physical therapist and certified in equine therapy. All our instructors who work with the program are fine horsemen and women and have taken courses in equine therapy.

"In addition to our riding instructors, we assign one of our employees—we call them buddies—to each teen for the month. They stick pretty closely to their assigned participant, and during the month *all* our hands are watching over them."

"Who are the other kids?" Lauren asked.

"Two boys and one other girl. All three have lost a parent and are struggling. We became involved after Reese donated some horses to a program run by veterans for veterans in Covenant Falls. They operate an ongoing program for veterans suffering from PTSD. They wanted to do one for kids who lost a military parent and/or had emotional or physical problems, but the demand for more veteran programs was too strong.

"In short, Reese wanted to help and decided to develop a program for kids of fallen military members. He assembled experts and came up with what we have now. We call them Junior Ranchers."

"I like that," Lauren said, "particularly giving each one a buddy."

"They are our younger cowhands who volunteer. They truly enjoy it and often stay in touch with their participant long after the program ends," Sally said.

"Tell me about the other participants," Lauren said.

"The boys are Heath Hanson, who lost a father in Afghanistan. He's currently living with his uncle. Tony Fields is the son of a veteran who had PTSD and committed suicide. The third is Jenny Jacobs. She lost her mother, a helicopter pilot, and her father isn't coping well.

"While they're here, they'll learn horsemanship and the care of horses. There is a psychologist—Dr. Paul Evans—who will drop in throughout the month. He's retired but keeps his credentials up-to-date, and he's like a grandfather to these kids.

"The kids learn to ride on well-trained riding horses," she continued. "There's any number of benefits. Riding improves balance, strengthens muscles and does wonders with self-confidence among other benefits. But with the mustangs, they just talk and spend time with them. The horses, in turn, learn to trust human beings. There seems to be some magic between these horses and youngsters with physical or emotional problems," Sally explained. "They both benefit."

"I read some books about it," Lauren asked. "Until

then I had no idea how many similar programs there are, and how valuable they can be."

"Horses by their very nature are empathetic. They want to please once they realize you're not going to harm them or their herd."

"How does the coed aspect work?"

"Fine. There's usually a healthy competition but these kids come from military families and are used to moving and making new friends. We talked about having all-girl and all-boy programs but then that would limit availability. So far it's worked well. They all have similar problems.

"We're very careful, though," she added. "The girls live in the house, the boys in the bunkhouse. In addition to the stables and an outside ring, we have a barn for storage and as a second riding ring in bad weather. We also have cameras throughout the property, and not only because of the program. Cattle rustling is still alive these days."

"And the mustangs?" Lauren asked as Sally refilled her glass with lemonade. The mustangs had been a major concern.

"There's nothing to worry about there," Sally said. "It's a matter of the kids talking to the horses from a safe distance. Maybe reading or singing to them. The kids prepare the horses for training by interacting with them, then watch as our horsemen start the training and finally become part of it. We've discovered the horses are far less nervous when 'their' person is present."

They finished the stew, and apple pie came next. Lauren was going to refuse but it smelled too good. It certainly was much better than her reheated frozen pies. If this was an example of what was served to the kids, she had no worries about the food aspect of the program.

When they finished lunch, Sally showed Lauren a scrapbook full of photos of previous participants and gave Lauren their parents' phone numbers if she wanted to check with them. "They've given us permission," she assured Lauren as she led Lauren and Bob to the room Julie would stay in. After that they went to the stable.

"Can I take photos with my cell?" Lauren asked.

"Sure. Anything you want," Sally said as she opened the door and led them down the aisle of stalls. Only a few stalls were occupied. "These are several of the riding horses used in the program," she said as they passed stalls. "Right here we have Snowflake, Anna Banana, Patches and Bandit, because of the black patches around his eyes. All are mustangs and were wild when they came to us. Now they're well-mannered saddle horses."

There was no mistaking Snowflake, who stuck out her head and whinnied a welcome. She was snow-white except for a few patches of black on her legs.

"She wants a carrot." Sally said. "There's some in that bucket near the door. Can you get four of them?"

Lauren did as requested. She gave two to Bob and they offered a carrot to each horse. Lauren started with Snowflake, who took a carrot gingerly and nuzzled Lauren's hand by way of thanks. She went to the next horse, a pinto named Patches, according to the sign attached to the door.

Just as they finished presenting the last carrot to Anna Banana, Sally's cell sang a happy tune, and she answered it. "Reese is coming through the gate. Would you like to see the unloading of the mustangs?"

Chapter 3

It was well after 1:00 p.m. when Reese reached the ranch, an hour late for his appointment with Mrs. MacInnes. As he drove slowly into the corral area, his foreman, Chet Hunter, jumped into the cab with him. "All set, boss. Food and water are in the paddock. The gate is open and the guys are ready to close it as soon as the horses are inside."

As Reese backed through the first gate, two hands closed it and followed the truck as Reese backed up to the second gate. Just as the rear of the trailer was inside the paddock, two ranch hands opened the back of the trailer and jumped out of the way as the horses hesitated, then, led by the black mare, charged out of the trailer and started galloping madly around the paddock. The burro stood in the middle, braying his annoyance over the situation.

Reese drove forward while the cowhands quickly closed the second gate. Chet jumped out of the cab and opened the first gate while Reese drove the trailer to the parking area.

He stepped out of the truck, and he and Chet went over to the paddock where the newcomers galloped madly around, trying desperately to find a way to escape. They would soon find the food and water already placed inside their new home and hopefully relax. The burro started to complain. It brayed. A very loud braying.

Reese still had no idea why he'd included the burro. But damn it, the little guy reminded him of Trouble, a burro his family owned when he was a kid. The name had been well-earned.

Chet looked at him. "A burro?"

"They threw him in for free."

Chet looked at him as if he'd grown a second head. "Boss, I know you like to save money but he's not exactly…free."

"I'll tell you a secret if you keep it that way."

Chet's eyes widened. "Hell, yeah."

"I kind of like burros," Reese admitted.

"No one likes burros. They're loud and bad-tempered."

"A moment of weakness," Reese said with a grin.

Reese gave a sigh of relief. The transfer from truck to paddock was always the most dangerous part of the process of bringing mustangs to the ranch, thus the double gates. He tried to bring them in at least three weeks before the equine therapy participants arrived. They would be calm enough then for the kids to work with them. At a safe distance.

His work would begin this afternoon, the long process of convincing the horses they had nothing to fear.

The kids would help and he'd watch them glow when a mustang took their first carrot from them, or immediately came over to the fence when they approached.

It was then he saw the woman and man walking toward him with Sally. Reese's attention went to the woman. She was a little taller than average. Athletic body. Short red hair—or was it copper?—framed a strong face. Watchful moss green eyes studied him. The man with her was of average height, a little shorter than his companion.

Reese took it all in within seconds before reaching out his hand. "Mrs. MacInnes, or is it Major MacInnes?"

"It's Lauren," she said as she clasped his hand in a firm handshake. "The major part ended a month ago." She paused, then added, "This is a friend, Major Bob Marsh. He flew me up from Texas."

Reese shook hands with him. "Welcome to Eagles' Roost. I apologize for being late, but an accident on the route slowed me up."

She glanced at the now closed doors of the stable. "It looked dangerous getting them into the paddock."

He raised an eyebrow. "That from a fighter pilot?"

"Planes don't kick and bite."

"But they get fired on," he said, "or run out of gas or have an electronic malfunction."

"Not if you know what you're doing."

"My point exactly," he said with a slight twist of his lips that might, just might, have been a smile. "I know what I'm doing. Just takes time and patience."

"Same thing about planes," she battled back.

"I suppose they both require respect," he said.

"And understanding," Lauren added.

They were sparring with each other, conversation

snapping between them. Their eyes met for what seemed a long time. An odd recognition flashed between them. It unnerved him and, he immediately sensed, did the same with her.

He didn't want more complications in his life. He was balancing balls like crazy. He didn't have time for a fleeting affair. Still, he guided her away from her companion and his sister and returned to the paddock where he could better observe the mustangs.

"You didn't bring your daughter with you," he said.

"No. I wanted to be sure it was...suitable before springing it on her. She's had a hard time. I didn't want to convince her into doing something that might be another disappointment."

"Whether or not it works depends on her," Reese said shortly. Damn it, he was tired and wanted nothing more than a glass of bourbon and a few hours of sleep. He didn't want to cross words with someone who was altogether too...attractive for his own good. He was willing to be pleasant but the *suitable* comment sort of got to him.

"We usually like more information and interviews," he continued with an edge in his voice. "But Patti was persuasive. If your daughter is eager to learn, she'll probably love it. Most kids do, after the first couple of days. There's usually a lot of fear in the beginning. It fades quickly and most fall in love with the horses within several days. But some do drop out. We don't promise miracles."

She raised an eyebrow, probably due to the impatience in his voice. "A miracle *would* be nice," she said, "but I'm not greedy. A smile would be a step forward." She paused, then asked, "How much did Patti tell you?"

"That a drunk driver killed your husband and badly injured your daughter, and that she's having a difficult time adjusting. She said both you and your husband were air force pilots, and that you were resigning your commission to be with her." He paused, seemed to weigh her, then added, "I expect that was difficult."

"It was and is," she admitted. "But it had to be done. I'm the only family she has now." She changed the subject. "Did Patti tell you that Julie was a runner, had just won a major race the night of the accident? That she blames me for being overseas at the time and herself for wanting to come back to the States and even for suggesting an ice cream the night of the crash?"

She stopped, shocked that the words had tumbled out. "I'm sorry," she said stiffly. "I don't usually sound off like that. It's just… I'm not used to…"

"Not being in control," he said. "I get it. I've been there." And he did know that feeling of helplessness. He knew it well. He'd felt it when he left Ag school midterm and suddenly became responsible for a ranch with thousands of cattle and forty employees, and then again twelve years later. He knew it only too well.

"Nothing to be sorry about. You and your daughter have a right to grieve. And be angry."

"Julie had such big dreams," Lauren said. "She was convinced she would make the Olympics in track and, frankly, she might have had a shot. She was that fast. Now she's not only lost a father she adored but also the dream they'd shared. She's still in a cast but that should be gone before coming here. She will have a brace, though. Would that be a problem?"

"Again, it depends on her. If she wants to be here, no. We've had amputees here and two kids in wheelchairs.

We've chosen our smartest and gentlest horses for this program and purchased equipment that will help the handicapped to mount. We have a horse that lies down while a rider boards her if necessary, and Sally can help with any exercises that are needed," he added. "I'm glad you met her. She's the heart and brains of this program in addition to bringing up a teenage son alone."

"Doesn't he have you?" she asked.

"An uncle isn't the same as a father." He saw the question in her eyes and was grateful her curiosity seemed to stop there.

"And the mustangs?" she asked. "Aren't they dangerous?"

"They're scared. Horses are prey animals. They seem to understand from the moment they're born that almost every other living thing wants to eat them. That includes man. They are usually born in the evening and are expected to run the next morning if necessary. It's nature's way of preserving the species. These horses probably had never seen a human being before a machine came from out of the sky and drove them from freedom into fences where they were separated from the herd that protected them since birth."

He knew he was being defensive, that he was lecturing, but he usually became incensed at the way the government was treating the wild horse population. That was not why she was here, though. She wanted to be assured her child wouldn't be injured.

"Why?" she asked, real interest in her voice.

"They usually seek out places that are uninhabited but they might wander too close to a farm or ranch and complaints are made to the US Department of Land Management. Then helicopters come in and drive the terrified animals to government-owned land, then to auctions."

"That doesn't sound right," she said, obviously identifying with the horses.

"I wish more people would agree," he said. "They are sold cheap and some buyers don't care what happens to them. The worse ones send them out of the country for horse meat. It's against the regulations but that doesn't mean much to some people. Some go to rodeos. Some go to legit buyers. We train them and make sure they go to good homes or we keep them for our own stock."

He stopped himself, then took a deep breath. "But to answer your question, the participants in our program won't be alone with a mustang, or even close to one until we're sure it's safe. Safety is our first concern," he continued. "We've never had a serious accident here."

He tried a smile through his weariness. He'd been up for three days with only a few hours of sleep. He rarely had much on such a trip. It had been a long drive to the auction, then a day of evaluating the horses and completing the paperwork involved, and finally loading terrified horses into his trailer before the long drive back.

As attractive—and interesting—as Lauren MacInnes was, he wanted to get back to the mustangs. Hopefully, they would have located the food and water by now. But he'd realized quickly his visitor needed reassurance. A lot of it.

He liked her for that. He would have felt the same way if his son had lived.

"When I heard about the program," she said, "I started reading books about equine therapy. I was surprised at the number and variety of programs being offered now."

"Because they work," he said. "There's something about horses that influences human behavior in a positive way. Maybe because they are so accepting. In the herd, they take care of the young and elderly. When gentled they do the same with humans. They don't abandon them as most species do when trouble approaches.

"Those scenes in Western films when the rider is injured, and the horse stays with him, well, they're accurate," he continued. "After these horses understand that humans won't hurt them, you give them a carrot and they think you're wonderful. It does great things for morale, particularly for a kid who feels no one understands."

He stopped. "Sorry about that," he said. "I'll get off my soapbox. What else do you want to know?"

"Your sister introduced us to some of the riding horses—Snowflake, Patches, Anna Banana and Bandit."

"They were named by the kids in the first session," he said with a grin. "We promised we would keep them, and it was much to the chagrin of my cowhands who ride them the other eleven months of the year. They prefer names like Thunder and Outlaw. Not a cowboy alive wants to ride a horse named Snowflake or Anna Banana. But then I suspect you know the breed."

She smiled for the first time. A real smile in those gorgeous eyes. "You think there was a wee bit of mischief involved in the naming?" she asked.

"I do," he replied. "I suspect pilots are a lot like cowboys, but a promise is a promise."

Her smile broadened. "I think you're right on both counts," she admitted.

"How far did you come today?" she asked.

"Couple of hundred miles. Usually six hours with

the trailer. Today it was eight. I hope it didn't mess up your schedule."

"Are they always in the same place?"

"No," he replied. "The sales are spread throughout the country, even in the South and eastern US. Whenever there's one within three hundred miles, I attend. Most mustangs go for a hundred and twenty-five dollars but some fine-looking ones go to auction. The black mare was one of them."

"I would like to go to one sometime."

He raised an eyebrow, then shrugged. "Easy to do. Just go to the Bureau of Land Management website. As I said, the sales move around the country. There's several held in Texas.

"Has Sally given you anything to eat?" He switched topics abruptly as he guided her back to where Bob stood talking to Sally.

"She did, and a fine lunch it was," Bob interjected. "I'm going to send my wife up here for cooking instructions."

One question was answered.

When he first saw the two together, he'd wondered if there was something between them. But apparently a flight up here was no more than offering a friend a ride to the grocery store for pilots. He had no idea why the thought that they might be more than friends bothered him. The last thing he needed now was an attractive woman with the greenest of eyes. "We feed a lot of people on the ranch, and they leave if the food's not good," Reese added. "We have a great cook."

She nodded. "I didn't give you much notice. But we should leave within the next hour. We want to get back to San Antonio before dark."

"Have you ever ridden horses?" He included both in the question again.

"No, although I've piloted some planes that felt like a bronc," she said while her companion shook his head.

Reese was intrigued. He hadn't known what to expect when told about her visit. Sally had made all the arrangements and had told him Mrs. MacInnes had been all business, even abrupt and obviously dubious about the program. Now he was discovering a quirky sense of humor when she allowed herself to relax.

"Sally also showed me the rooms she would share with another girl."

"Jenny Jacobs. She's shy but excited."

"Exactly how does it work, once she gets here?" Lauren asked.

"When your daughter arrives, if she decides to come, she'll pick one of our trained horses you saw earlier in the stables on the left side of the house."

"Snowflake?" Lauren said impishly.

He grinned. "We'll see. We try to let the kids pick their horse. But I'll be sure she has one that will work for her and her leg, and we also have steps that can help."

He went on, while Sally continued to chat with Bob. "She'll also get a female buddy—one of our young female ranch hands—who will stay with her throughout the program. She's there as a friend to answer questions, teach basic horsemanship and root her on.

"The four buddies are full-time employees with us and volunteer to do this. They're young enough to remember how it was at their age and usually connect easily to *their* kid. They'll teach them about the horses, how to make friends with them and how to groom and saddle them. They'll help our full-time riding instructors, a US champion barrel racer and my sister, who is an expert rider herself. Like me, she's been on a horse since she was four or five."

He added, "Three of my hands have been trained as equine therapy certified."

He hesitated as he saw the doubt in her face. "The kids learn horsemanship in the morning and in the afternoon spend time with their mustang. Chet, my foreman, and I supervise contact between the mustangs and our participants.

"There's no touching for a week or so—it depends on the horse. Maybe longer. Maybe less. Depends on how it goes."

He paused. "If all goes well, we start the next stage. When the horse starts coming over to her, she'll give him a treat. Might be a carrot or an apple. She will be showing the mustang it has nothing to fear from humans, and a young person is less threatening than an older one. Then, typically, the horse begins to trust. One of our horse wranglers will teach the horse basic manners like how to walk on a lead, but our participant will continue to be its friend, the one that makes it easier for our wrangler. As the relationship strengthens, our student gains confidence as well as a new friend."

He was tired and he knew he wasn't at his best. He was being a little short, and she didn't deserve that when she'd come a long distance to help her daughter.

Lauren MacInnes tipped her head. "And if it doesn't go well?"

"We occasionally have a mustang that doesn't respond but that's unusual. If that occurs, then we'll concentrate on building her, or his, riding skills with trusted horses."

"What if she and her roommate don't get along?"

"They'll learn to. For the time she's here, she'll be part of a family," he said. "They'll eat together, learn together, exercise together, have small and large successes together. Usually, the initial shyness fades away."

Just then a big black-and-white dog bounded out of nowhere to jump on him, making whining noises. Lauren was quick enough to take a photo.

"I've just been gone four days," he told the dog, then turned to her. "Excuse his behavior. This is Leo."

"Hello, Leo," she said.

Leo offered his paw.

She looked at Reese.

"He wants you to shake it," he said.

She did.

"Now you've been accepted. He looks after everyone who is here. There are three other dogs, including two cattle dogs, but Leo is king of the Roost."

She raised an eyebrow at the description, and he liked the fact that she got his pitiful sense of humor. "Julie always wanted a dog," Lauren said.

"You're going to spoil him," Reese warned her as she leaned down and ran her hands through his thick fur.

"He looks spoiled already."

"He's a ranch dog," he disagreed. "Chases varmints."

"What kind of varmints?"

"Snakes. Prairie dogs that dig holes that could injure both rider and horse, an occasional mountain lion or bear that comes down from the mountains."

"Are you trying to scare me, Mr. Howard?"

"That would be rather useless, wouldn't it?" he said. "I doubt a fighter pilot is afraid of a snake or even a bear."

"You would be wrong," she replied and changed the

subject. "Can I take a photo of him with his paw up? I took several of the horses. It might be the winning ticket with my daughter."

"Sure. Leo would be more than pleased. He loves attention."

"In addition to chasing varmints?" she said.

"Yep," he said. He liked that quirky sense of humor that poked out once in a while. It softened the barrier that was evident in the first moments of their meeting. But then he hadn't been particularly welcoming.

"What's the rule about parents?" she asked. "Can I stick around while Julie is here? If, that is, I can get her to come."

"We ask that you don't visit for the first week. Some kids want to leave on the first day but on the fourth you can't pry them away. The idea is to immerse them in ranch activities. There will be some chores such as feeding the horses and grooming them. We like to make it as much of a typical day on any ranch as we can.

"After that first week, you're welcome to visit on Sundays," he added. "But let us know so it won't interfere with a lesson."

Lauren nodded. "I understand that. I've been with her every day since the accident. She'd always been adventuresome before that. Now she has nightmares and doesn't want anyone to see she needs a cast or brace."

He nodded. "We'll brief the staff, particularly your daughter's buddy, on everything you've told us. We've had lots of experience with trauma."

There was something in his voice that told her he knew about trauma. "Tell me about the horses you brought in," she said.

"They're scared now," he said. "They don't know

what is happening. Many of them have never had contact with people."

"That's sad," she said. "From what I can see of them, they look…active," Lauren said.

"*Active* is one word for it. Another is *panicked*. But with good food, a lot of patience and grooming they'll look and act a lot better."

"I wasn't aware there were many wild mustangs in the country."

"Not many people are. There's still a lot of empty land throughout the country. Herds seem very adept at finding places to graze. They eat what's there, then move on. They're very wise about that. Problem is when a herd *is* sighted, they're rounded up and driven to places that often don't have enough natural resources to maintain them or they're driven to auctions. We're losing our heritage." Indignation put a bite into his words. He shrugged self-consciously. "I get carried away sometimes."

"I hope it's catching," Lauren said wistfully. "Julie used to be curious, but now she's reluctant to even go outside. She's very self-conscious about using crutches, although she's had an operation that we hope will solve that problem."

"That usually wears off fast around here when her companions all have had disasters of their own," he said. He was finding it more and more difficult not to meet those eyes directly. They were just too damn brilliant. Why hadn't Patti warned him?

"She's gone through hell. Four operations. Once a whirling dervish, now she rarely leaves the house—except for medical reasons. She's been mourning her father and blaming herself for the accident while undergoing multiple surgeries on her leg. We're waiting to see whether the last one will be *the* last one.

"It would give her some control over her left foot," Lauren continued. "Right now she doesn't feel as if she has control over anything. But Patti says her favorite books involve horses and other animals so I'm crossing fingers that this program will help bring back the old Julie."

When Lauren MacInnes smiled, her face lit. He realized now that her multitude of questions had not been personal but because she was someone used to making decisions and now found herself floundering in quicksand.

Reese turned to Bob. "Ever been in this area before?"

"No, I had no idea there were ranches in the mountains." The man paused, then added, "You have some operation here. How many cattle do you have?"

"Damn if I know exactly," Reese said. He ignored what was considered the ultimate no-no in cattle culture of never asking a cowman how many cattle he had. He chalked it up to ignorance. "We'll have a new count in the spring when the calves come, but it's several thousand."

"That's a bunch to look after," Bob said.

"Yeah, it is," Reese said, suddenly impatient to get that glass of whiskey and visit the mustangs. He was too attracted to Mrs. MacInnes and far too quickly. "I should get back to the mustangs," he said.

A sudden very loud braying interrupted the conversation. All four of them glanced back at the paddock.

"*What* was that?" Bob asked.

"It's a burro," Reese said with a slight smile. "He's hidden in there among the mustangs."

Bob looked puzzled. "A burro?"

"Another word for donkey but usually a smaller—and louder—version. They're the offspring of a mare and a donkey and are called donkey in the East and burro in the West. They're often found with a herd of horses and this one was rounded up with this group of mustangs. He was thrown in the package for free because no one else would take him. He's a loud little critter. Bossy, too. Don't know what in the hell we'll do with him."

Lauren glanced up at him, as if seeing through his words and knowing the burro was probably going nowhere. Their gazes held. He couldn't look away. There was a connection, a flash of understanding that went soul deep. He was stunned by it.

"I think we should start back," Bob said, breaking that thin thread that had passed between him and Lauren MacInnes.

Reese jerked back to reality as Lauren nodded.

"Did we pass inspection?" Reese asked with a half smile.

"If you will have her."

"Patti would never talk to me again if I didn't say yes," Reese said. "And next to Sally and Nathan, my nephew, she's my favorite person. I respect the hell out of her. I offered to help her with her tuition, and she turned me down."

"Why?"

He shrugged, but she gave him a suspicious look.

Lauren held out her hand. "Thanks. I think this would be great for Julie. All I have to do is convince *her.*"

He shook her hand for a brief second, nodded and turned around with Leo at his heels.

* * *

Lauren stared after him. She recognized avoidance gestures when she saw them. There was a story there, somewhere, where Patti and her tuition were concerned. She suspected there were a lot of stories around the ranch.

Sally said, "He's always like this when new mustangs come in, and I doubt whether he had any sleep last night. He usually doesn't at one of these auctions. Can't keep him away from them. He'll be down there singing to the mustangs this evening."

"Singing?" Lauren asked.

She nodded. "Along with some of the guys. Reese believes it relaxes the horses."

"And do you believe it?" Lauren asked.

"Yep. Just like it does with cattle. I even join in sometimes except my voice seems to scare them."

"What about his?"

"It's actually pretty good," Sally said.

Another interesting fact about him. "You said *guys*," Lauren said, "but he mentioned female hands."

"Being a ranch hand is a hard, dirty job that takes a lot of strength," Sally replied. "I worked with the horses as a kid but I didn't do the heavy stuff. But out of about forty, we have five women and they're among the best. Two of them have come out of the Horses for Heroes program near Covenant Falls."

Patti had mentioned Covenant Falls. Maybe she could explore that area if Julie was here.

A big *if*. Now that she felt more confident about the program, she would still have to convince Julie.

Sally smiled. "I hope to see your daughter here. It

sounds like she's had a rough time, but horses and kids go together. There's a lot of magic between them."

As she drove the rental car back to the plane, Lauren tried to absorb everything she'd seen.

And felt.

Damn it, she'd been drawn to the tall, rangy rancher and she couldn't figure out how it had happened. It was the first time in a year and a half that her heart quickened when she was with a guy. She never even imagined she would—or could—feel even the slightest attraction for another man after Dane died.

Physically, they were quite different. Dane had been shorter, leaner, and his clipped hair was blond where Reese Howard's was dark, almost black and, truth be told, a bit shaggy. A shock of it had fallen over his forehead, and he'd run his fingers through it, pushing it back in place.

Reese was tall, rangy in build, but every movement seemed to have a grace to it. He was not handsome in a classic way, but there was a rugged attractiveness that appealed to her. His cheekbones were high and his mouth was wide, sensual and curved in a reserved smile. Reese Howard had the same intensity as Dane and obviously the same commitment to what they did for a living although their jobs—their lives—were worlds apart: Dane flying the most advanced aircraft in the world, and Reese Howard more comfortable in the saddle.

But she wasn't ready yet to entertain thoughts of another man, nor, she was sure, would Julie be ready for that, either. Patti had forgotten to mention her cousin was a bachelor, which he apparently was. There had been no mention of a wife or child. Nor had Patti mentioned the size of the ranch and the big, rambling ranch house that had obviously undergone constant growth.

It was a far different world than hers. If she were smart, she would run like all the demons in hell chased her, but the program and change of scenery could help her daughter, and that was all that was important.

Chapter 4

They were halfway back to San Antonio before either Bob or Lauren spoke. The cockpit didn't encourage conversation. He'd been busy with flying, and she tried to absorb everything she'd heard and seen, particularly her reaction to Reese Howard.

Lauren had been wary of the program when she'd arrived. She wasn't going to leave her daughter with a stranger without knowing more. She'd done due diligence and asked the navy psychologist to check Eagles' Roost out. His report was positive, even glowing.

But that was not enough. She'd had to see it for herself. Her first impression was poor when Reese Howard was late for their appointment.

She liked Sally Reynolds. Still, she planned to contact the parents of past participants. It was that pilot's training again. You check everything once, twice and three times.

The ranch was far larger than she'd anticipated, and the ranch house was intriguing. According to Sally, it had been built in 1910 after the original was destroyed in a fire. As the family multiplied, additions were built, but the house, though sprawling, looked comfortable. For someone who had lived in a three-room apartment in a poor neighborhood for years, then military housing, it was…impressive.

But her main goal had been to meet the man in charge. For some reason she'd expected someone older, someone more…

More what?

He'd looked rough, disheveled and tired when he arrived. He certainly didn't look like someone who owned thousands of cattle. He had two or three days of beard but his dark, almost black eyes were intelligent and wary. His jeans and jean jacket were stained. He wasn't handsome in traditional terms, but he would be hard to ignore in a crowd.

It was the unexpected humor and lack of ego that attracted her as he walked her around the ranch area. He'd been curt in the beginning, obviously eager to get back to the mustangs, but he'd relaxed as he talked about his love of the mustangs, the ranch and his equine therapy program.

The ranch awakened her childhood longings. She'd been an avid reader as a child and practically lived in the library when she wasn't helping her mother. Among her favorite books were those about animals. Animals and adventures. Even at six, she'd wanted to have adventures.

Maybe she could give her daughter one. An adventure that would awaken her fighting spirit.

"What do you think?" she asked Bob through their

headphones as they approached the airport near San Antonio. She wondered if meeting Reese Howard was affecting her judgment.

"I think Howard's for real," he said as if reading her mind. "Sounds like a great program to me."

"You think it's safe, then?"

"I watched the way they brought in those mustangs. Howard obviously knows what he's doing. Everything about the ranch says good management—the way they handled the mustangs, the cleanliness of the stables and the other buildings. He doesn't have to do this equine therapy program. Doesn't bring him anything but satisfaction. But he's a man who expects results. I think it would be good for Julie."

His observations only strengthened her instincts. She had been dubious about the idea, but the ranch stirred something in her. The only problem now was to stir it in Julie, as well.

"Thanks for flying me down there," she said.

"Dane would have done the same for my wife and I would do it for any coworker."

"I'm not a coworker any longer," she said sadly.

"You will be once Julie gets her life together. She's completely dependent on you, or thinks she is. This horse thing is her chance to regain some independence."

"If she agrees to attend…"

"She will, and I know for a fact the air force would like you back in a New York minute."

Lauren wished she was as optimistic as Bob was. The four of them—Dane, herself, Bob and Sue—had been friends for nearly all the time they'd served in the air force. Bob had been in training with Dane and had been his best man at their wedding. Lauren had been maid of honor for Sue. They babysat for each other when they were in Germany together.

Unfortunately, her thoughts returned to the ranch's owner. She'd been irritated until he stepped down from the trailer and watched as the horses dashed down into the paddock or corral. He looked as if he belonged to those mountains that surrounded the ranch. Rugged and formidable.

He'd been both impatient and empathetic. He'd obviously wanted to get back to the newly arrived horses but he was just as obviously committed to the program for kids. There was humor lurking in him as well, as he talked to and about Leo and the burro.

Patti had said he was one fourth Ute, which may have accounted for his black hair and dark eyes. She wasn't usually wowed by appearances. She didn't trust them. But there was something about the intensity in the man's face as they met that turned her common sense upside down. Electricity had struck her, run down her spine. She knew that intensity had nothing to do with her. It had been the horses. But for some crazy reason, it awakened a part of her she thought numb inside. It reminded her of the excitement she'd felt on her first flight.

She recognized it but didn't understand.

She gave up trying to do that as they arrived at the private airfield in San Antonio where Bob's group parked their plane.

Julie's big toe finally wriggled two days after Lauren arrived home. The operation had worked.

The simple act of moving one large toe probably meant no more surgeries. There would be more weeks in a brace and with crutches as the fragile muscles and bone grew stronger. The leg would never be as good as it once was, but the threat of losing it had declined substantially. Some of its mobility would be lost but with time, according to the doctors, she would have an almost normal walk.

"You did it! I knew you would," Lauren said. "We'll celebrate with a cake. You made it happen!"

"I did, didn't I?" Julie replied with one of the few smiles Lauren had seen in months.

"So what about taking that trip to Colorado?" Lauren asked. Time was becoming her enemy. Julie had been too concerned with those toes to even consider the program.

"I could hurt the leg." Julie still resisted.

"I don't think so," Patti said. "You'll be safe. Believe me, I wouldn't even suggest it if I thought there was a chance it wasn't."

"And," Lauren added, "your doctor thinks it's a terrific idea. Think of it as a vacation. You certainly deserve one and it's beautiful up there. You'll love the horses and Leo the dog."

The mention of the dog seemed to swing it. Julie had almost smiled when she saw the photo of Leo holding out a paw as if inviting her to come. "I would have to go through airports," Julie said. "Everyone will be looking at me."

"Because you're a very pretty girl," Patti said.

Julie gave her a disgusted look.

Lauren jumped in. "Bob or Jim Harris will fly us up and I'll rent a car. Or else we can drive all the way. Take a prolonged road trip." She looked at her daughter. "You haven't been out of the house except for doctor visits."

Julie didn't reply, but at least she didn't say no. That

was progress. She'd been hiding from everyone. She thought she was ugly because of a narrow line scar on her forehead. It was almost invisible but to Julie it was huge. The good news was the cast was due to come off. The bad news was she would still need braces and crutches for a while. The new braces would have a shoe attached to stabilize the foot. To someone who had loved the freedom of running, it was still a prison sentence. Today's news about the toes, though, meant she shouldn't need them too long.

Lauren waited with bated breath. It had to be Julie's decision. Sally had known that and agreed. After one of the youngsters dropped out of the program, it was too late to find another applicant. If it had not been for Patti, it would have been too late for Julie, as well.

"I can leave after the first three days?" Julie asked, clearly wanting reassurance. "What if I want to come home sooner?"

"It's not jail, sweetie. They ask that you stay three days but no one's going to chain you there." Lauren would promise anything to get a sparkle back in those dark blue eyes. "It's not a dude ranch or anything like that. It's a working ranch. It's authentic and in a beautiful location."

"Is Patti going? She's a relative, isn't she?"

"You'll have to ask her."

Julie turned to Patti. "Will you?"

"Afraid not, Julie. I have to do some work before returning to the university. But maybe one weekend I can manage it. I would love to visit the ranch again. I worked there one summer, and I love it. You will, too."

"Okay," Julie said dubiously as she scanned photos of the horses and Leo. "If you promise I don't have to stay after three days if I don't like it?"

"Promise," Lauren pledged.

Lauren left the room and went out to the kitchen. She looked at the framed photo of Dane she kept on a counter there. He had a cocky smile that belied the perfectionist inside. "She's going to be okay," she told him. "I was worried about her for a while, but now…now maybe she will come out of that shell."

She cut three thick slices of a cake she'd bought yesterday. Julie was much too thin. Once a good eater because it fueled her running, she now picked at her food. Before the accident, Lauren would have added ice cream, but now the very words still brought tears from Julie.

"When would we go?" Julie asked.

"A week from now."

"How?"

"We'll figure that out. And," she added, "we'll have to go shopping for clothes. You'll need some pants."

Julie's eyes clouded again. "How can I wear them with the brace?" she said. Because of the bulky cast, she'd been limited to skirts or, at home, loose robes. The brace wouldn't be much better.

"I've been thinking about that," she said. "What about some gaucho pants? They're very fashionable."

Julie's eyes widened. "Fashionable?"

Lauren would find some if it was the last thing she did. She'd seen gaucho pants in fashion ads. They shouldn't be too hard to find. Mental note: check the internet.

After finishing the celebratory cake, Patti left for the apartment she now shared with a roommate. The house felt empty without her. Patti would be leaving in the fall and Lauren didn't know what she would do without her. What Julie would do. She was part of Lauren's family now. Including Patti, there were three of them. Neither she nor Dane had extended family or at least one that would acknowledge Dane's existence. Lauren had tried to call Dane's family before the funeral. They were in Europe. She'd sent a letter to the only address she knew, telling them of Dane's death and their granddaughter's injury. It was also ignored.

What kind of father—and mother—would disown a son because he didn't follow in the family business? Not only a son but a granddaughter.

Julie had asked about them in the past few months. Lauren only replied that she couldn't reach them.

Dane's father had disowned him when Dane dropped out of business school to join the air force. Several attempts on Dane's part to contact them were rebuffed and he finally gave up. She didn't want her daughter to undergo her father's disappointments.

Perhaps the prospect of wild mustangs and a dog who liked to say hello would quiet her longing for more family.

In the end it *was* the photos of Leo the dog and the mustangs that lured Julie to Eagles' Roost. Lauren threw in the promise of a permanent dog to clinch the deal. They'd debated different ways of traveling—plane, train or automobile—and finally settled on the last. Lauren had planned to stay in the area for a week or so and would need a car. It seemed simpler to drive up there.

The first day was long and hard. They left at six in the morning with the objective of reaching the Colorado border by nightfall. Julie was obviously apprehensive, but Lauren asked her to pick the place they'd have their overnight stay, and her daughter's natural curiosity kicked in as they traveled north through cattle country and she started asking more questions about Eagles' Roost.

When they reached Raton, on the New Mexico–Colorado border, Julie had already decided on a funky historic spot she found online. She'd wanted to stay in a bed-and-breakfast rather than a motel and she chose an old rooming house that had been converted.

The rooms were small, especially the bathroom, but the building overlooked a fast-running river and was surrounded by aspens in their golden glory. Julie had traveled in the mountains in Germany, but the Raton Pass was far different with its cragged peaks and wildflowers and aspens.

Breakfast was excellent: strawberry pancakes and a bowl of fresh fruit with pastries.

"I wish we could stay here," Julie said longingly as they left the bed-and-breakfast. "It's so…peaceful. Can't we stay longer?"

Lauren feared it was more an excuse not to reach the ranch with new people and expectations than love of the wilderness.

"It's just as scenic there," Lauren said as she drove onto the road. "Along with horses and dogs and even a burro."

She hoped the mention would stir her daughter's curiosity but instead Julie lapsed into silence.

She looked at her clock on the dashboard and realized they were running late. Hopefully, she could make up some time.

Lauren sensed Julie was growing increasingly nervous and uncertain as they approached the ranch. Even fearful, which was totally unlike her. Until the accident, she'd been fearless.

Lauren was just as nervous. Julie had been her life since the accident. She had no idea what she was going to do with herself, not only now or in three days or three weeks but in the months and years ahead once Julie recovered. She'd promised Julie she wouldn't rejoin the air force although an invitation was there for her to do so.

There was nothing else she wanted to do, nothing else she was qualified for, and she'd never been idle before. Now she faced weeks of idleness. Maybe that was why she'd been unable to shove Reese Howard from her mind since she'd met him.

Just like pilots were intense about flying, he was equally as intense about his mustangs and ranch, probably in that order. But pilots also knew how to relax. She doubted whether Reese Howard did.

She'd pumped Patti. It was obvious she adored her cousin.

According to Patti, he had grown up working on the ranch. He'd learned to ride at five and worked with the ranch hands at fourteen. But when his father was disabled, the ranch had been a lot for a twenty-year-old to manage. "He'd not only managed," Patti had claimed, "but the ranch flourished under him. Unlike most ranches today, Eagles' Roost rarely lost an employee. He never asked them to do something he didn't do, including mucking the stables."

Stop thinking about him. She shuddered to think Julie might read her mind. The very attraction was disloyal to Dane.

Just then the traffic slowed to a crawl, and it wasn't until three miles and forty-five minutes later that she learned why. There had been a rockslide and traffic was limited to one lane. Somebody, she thought, was trying to tell her something.

She recalled her reaction to Reese Howard's tardiness and winced. She was going to have to eat some serious crow.

Chapter 5

Reese was on hand to greet the families as they brought their teens to Eagles' Roost. He knew the backgrounds and, except for Julie, had met both parents and teens.

Jenny Jacobs, fourteen, and her father were the first to arrive. The second was sixteen-year-old Tony Fields, whose veteran father had committed suicide after years of PTSD. His mother and her fiancé brought him. The third was Heath Hanson, fifteen, who'd lost his father in Afghanistan. His aunt and uncle drove him to the ranch.

There was no sign of the fourth: Lauren MacInnes and her daughter.

He spent the next hour introducing the teens and their families to the rest of the staff and especially to the teens' buddies for the duration of the program.

As he introduced a buddy to each teen, he explained their role in the program. They would help them choose a horse, teach basic care of their mount, answer questions about riding and ranch life. Most of all, they were to be a friend, someone who had their back.

Experienced riding instructors would take over riding lessons Monday, but the buddy would remain to cheer them on and solve any problem that otherwise might arise between the participants.

Reese was particularly proud that many of those relationships continued after the program ended. Two of the previous kids returned to hire on at the ranch after high school graduation, and both were buddies today. Reese had recently attended the high school graduation of one of the early participants who received a full university scholarship.

Heath's uncle drew Reese aside. "Heath is…withdrawn. He's been moved around a lot."

"I matched him with a buddy who is a former Junior Rancher and had that same problem. He understands and will let Heath go at his own pace. You would be surprised how much a horse will help."

He looked over at the boy who had wandered over to one of the paddocks. "We're having a bonfire and variety show tonight," he added. "It features some of our ranch hands. They all go to extremes to win a vote at the end. There's nothing like a terrible comic to make you laugh. It always breaks the ice with the kids," he added.

But even as he reassured the parents, he watched for a redhead with a daughter.

Jenny's father came over to him. "I thought there was another girl," he said.

"They're running late," he said, hoping it was true. He just didn't see Lauren MacInnes dropping out without notifying him. Certainly, Patti would have known.

When the last parent left and the kids were escorted to

the stables to meet the horses and learn the first elements of horsemanship, he checked his cell. No messages. Disappointment flooded him. Mrs. MacInnes must have changed her mind, or her daughter had changed hers.

He walked over to the mustangs' stable. Now that the crowd had dispersed, he released them into the paddock and watched them gallop around the perimeter. It was a handsome group now that they were filling out. True to the nature of a burro, Mistake, as Reese had named him, trotted along with them, kicking one, then hiding behind another.

But even the mustangs didn't lessen the disappointment that went deep. He hadn't been able to banish Lauren MacInnes from his thoughts since she'd visited Eagles' Roost three weeks earlier and was looking forward to seeing her again today. Maybe that first attraction was superficial but he hadn't felt anything close to it in years.

She was a pretty woman. He could ignore that, but there was so much more to her than that: a wry sense of humor, sharp intelligence and an obvious interest in everything around her, including his mustangs.

No matter how hard he tried, he couldn't erase the image of those vivid green eyes. It hadn't helped that Patti called several times and updated him on the mother and daughter. Patti could be very critical of people if they didn't live up to her standards, but she couldn't say enough about Lauren and her devotion to her daughter. Strong. Smart. Caring. The two had obviously become friends during the summer.

Mrs. MacInnes was usually the type of woman he avoided. He'd discovered, painfully, that a woman needed more than he could give. The ranch came first.

It had been that way since the day his father was thrown from a horse. He couldn't go on a vacation or even plan a dinner without the possibility that a mare would give birth, or a cow was sick or a dozen other emergencies.

Then five years ago he responded to a plea for the loan of horses for a veteran equine therapy program in Covenant Falls some one hundred miles away. He'd donated several horses and loaned them more.

It was there he learned there was also a need for a program that helped kids who'd either lost a military parent or who suffered because of a parent's mental or physical wounds due to combat. There were a growing number of programs for adult veterans but few for the young victims of war.

He'd studied other programs, talked to experts, gathered the assistance of professionals and plunged ahead. His sister was an equine therapy–trained physical therapist and he enlisted a semiretired psychologist from the valley. Three of his employees took equine therapy training, as well.

Now the participants had become *his* kids.

Reese was self-aware enough to realize he had wounds of his own that affected his way of molding the program. He'd never had a childhood. His father had raised him to take over the ranch, just as Reese's grandfather had raised his son. There were no after-school activities or summer vacations. The only trips were to buy horses or cattle or feed or other ranch necessities.

But the horses made up for it. He'd always had a way with them. Even his father had to admit that his system was better than the old way of breaking them. Reese talked to them, let them know him, and slowly introduced them to the bridle and the harness and the saddle.

He knew horses could heal people, and he wanted others to understand it, too. He loved Winston Churchill's comment about horses: "The outside of a horse is good for the inside of a man." It had been that way for him. He wanted to share it.

From what Patti told him about Lauren's daughter, he felt it was exactly what Julie MacInnes needed.

He didn't like being wrong. He would have bet a hefty sum that she'd believed Junior Ranchers would help her daughter. She'd sent all the pertinent information, including medical records and a psychologist's report.

Damn it, stop wallowing in disappointment. He had his mustangs to feed. Horses were a lot less complicated than women. *Feed them. Talk to them. Take care of them. They're your friends for life.*

He headed for the house when he saw his bookkeeper/business manager drive up. He'd forgotten she was dropping by today to finish some work before leaving for Chicago first thing in the morning. Her mother had had a heart attack and she didn't know how long she would be there.

Sandra Lewis was an electronic genius in addition to being his bookkeeper. He lived in fear that someday he might lose her. He hated being trapped in an office, and he was electronically inept. Fortunately, Sandra was married to the owner of the small local bank and liked keeping busy.

"Hi, Reese," she said as he accompanied her inside his office and they both sat down at the computer.

They had gone through several feed bills and he'd electronically signed a contract when Sally entered and interrupted him. "Just had a call from your missing family," she said. "They should be here in a few minutes.

Apparently, they had a late start, then took the road with the rockslide. No cell service, of course. She was very apologetic." She raised an eyebrow. "It's just an hour later than you were three weeks ago," she reminded him.

He had to grin at the comment. Sally was six years younger and grew up under the same tyrannical father who became even more so after his accident.

Reese always tried to protect her from their father's tantrums, especially after the injury, but she'd fled the day she finished high school and become pregnant by a no-good charmer. She'd waited until their father died before coming home with a son but no husband. In that time his little sister had grown up and they made a good team. She could ride as well as he and was a fantastic cook.

"Robin and I will wait for them while you finish with Sandra," Sally offered and hurried out before he could protest.

Sandra made out a to-do list for him while she was gone. He raised an eyebrow at its length and groaned.

"I should be back within the week," she said. "You'll be fine," she assured him as she left, leaving him still staring at the list.

Julie had grown increasingly antsy and uncertain as she and Lauren neared Eagles' Roost Ranch. Lauren was just as nervous.

"It looks big," Julie said as they finally reached the ranch and started down the road toward the large house and two stables, one on each side of the road.

"It is," Lauren replied. "They have several thousand cattle along with a lot of horses." She tried to keep her voice steady but she was wondering whether she was making the right decision bringing her daughter here.

Every time she looked at the sky she yearned to be up there. There was nothing else she wanted to do, nothing else she was qualified for, and she'd never been idle before.

"Do you really think the gaucho pants look okay?" Julie's question jerked her back to the minute as she parked in the large lot. Lauren had found them online and bought three pairs for Julie and one for herself. Julie approved when her items arrived and slipped easily over her brace while fitting the rest of her slim form perfectly. "You don't think they look odd?" Her daughter worried now.

"I think they look terrific," Lauren said. And they did. Lauren had found some leather ones, and they looked fashionably Western. She worried about boots that had been on the essentials list for the program, but there was nothing she could do about that with the brace and support shoe.

The parking lot had some of the same vehicles as before but no new ones. She parked in the area in front of the house.

Sally must have been watching for them. She and a young woman in a Western shirt, riding pants and boots stepped from the porch and approached the car. Lauren stepped outside and opened the back door for Julie, who had been resting her bad leg on the backseat.

"You must be Julie," Sally said as Julie twisted around to get the leg in the brace and crutches out of the car. "Welcome to Eagles' Roost. I'm Sally." She turned to a young woman next to her. "This is Robin. She's usually a ranch hand—one of the best we have and one of the few women—but during this month she'll be working exclusively with you. She'll introduce you to the horses and teach you about ranch life. If you need anything or have any questions, she's the person to ask."

Robin smiled widely as she reached out and shook Julie's hand. "Welcome to Eagles' Roost. You're going to have a great adventure. Promise."

Even Julie couldn't resist Robin's contagious smile. She nodded as she awkwardly stepped out of the car. Just then a large black-and-white dog loped over to the car and sniffed Julie before swiping a wet tongue over the hand that was on the crutch.

"This is Leo," Sally said to Julie. "He doesn't have any manners, but he adores everyone and expects adoration in return. Robin will take your luggage to your room while I introduce you to the other participants. They're in the barn getting their first lesson in horsemanship."

Julie didn't move and Lauren ached for her. Before the accident, Lauren would have appreciated Julie's need to be close to her. Now Lauren wished her daughter felt safe and confident enough not to need her nearby. She was fifteen now, and Lauren wanted her to be like other teenagers. She even wanted to worry about her daughter coming home a few minutes late from a party.

But no more than a few minutes.

Sally tried again with Julie. "Is that okay with you?"

Julie looked overwhelmed but the fact that Sally gave her daughter permission to make her own decision did the trick. Julie nodded.

"I'll take care of your luggage and meet you inside the barn," Robin said. "And I love those pants. You're going to have to tell me where to find them. They're cool."

The comment drew a rare smile from Julie.

"We'll have fun together," Robin assured her.

Julie didn't look so sure but at least she was reaching for the door handle to help her balance as she stepped out of the car. Lauren went to the back of the car, opened the trunk and pointed out Julie's belongings: a packed suitcase, a satchel containing her purse, her laptop and an e-reader with a wealth of books waiting inside.

Lauren hadn't figured on such a quick goodbye but maybe it was best. A little devil inside had looked forward to seeing Reese Howard again. But it was probably just as well. He'd been in her thoughts too frequently.

She hugged Julie for a moment. In truth, she wanted to grab her daughter and drive away. "I'm as close as a phone call," she said instead. "Have a great time."

"She'll be fine when she feels the soft muzzle of a horse and looks into big brown eyes," Sally said.

Lauren hugged Julie. "Enjoy. I love you," she said. "You have my cell number. Call anytime," she said despite the recommendation of no phone calls for three days. She stepped away and watched as Robin headed for the house while Sally, her daughter and Leo walked slowly toward the barn. Her daughter looked rigid. She turned around and looked back; her features seemed to be begging her not to go, then she walked into the barn.

Lauren blinked away tears. She felt as if she was throwing her daughter off a cliff without a safety net.

Reese left the house as Lauren MacInnes watched her daughter disappear into the stable with Sally and Leo. He walked toward her and as he neared, she turned, startled. The vivid green he remembered was misted with tears. She tried to blink them back when she saw him. Damn, those emerald eyes could lead to a man's downfall.

She took a step back as he approached. The vulnerability touched him. "You made it," he said. "I thought you might have changed your mind."

She shook her head. "I wouldn't do that without letting you know. But I'll never be able to complain about you being late again," she replied.

"You didn't exactly do that," he said. "It was just cool indignation."

"Okay," she shot back. "We're even. You ran into a gas truck on the road. I ran into a rockslide. Do you think someone is trying to tell us something?"

"Could be," he said with a grin. "You must have come the long way, then," he said. "Those rocks have been there a long time."

"It looked like a shortcut on the map," she said wryly. "I really dislike being late. It's a military thing."

"I rather guessed that. Did you drive all the way from San Antonio?"

"I did. We started at dawn yesterday. Julie wants me to stay around close for a while. It was a condition. Seven hundred miles seems a long way to her. Your sister recommended an inn in Covenant Falls."

"Your daughter wants a quick getaway option?"

"Something like that."

"She's not alone. I think all four of the kids have those doubts today, but they usually disappear fairly quickly." He paused, then added, "I saw your daughter walk to the barn. She seems to manage well on those crutches."

"She shouldn't need them more than another week. She's getting used to walking with the brace. Hopefully, she won't need that long."

"That's good news."

Lauren nodded but bit her lip, and he realized how

difficult it had been to bring her daughter. "I know now why you were late that day. I didn't realize from the air how winding the roads are. I should have."

"It's even and forgotten," he said. "I suppose Sally explained the buddy system. Robin was one of the first kids to come here to Junior Ranchers," he said. "She knows how scary it can be."

"And she came back?"

"As a ranch hand during the summers. She learned to ride here, and now she's earning money to go to college. She wants to become a veterinarian."

"She lost a parent, too?"

He nodded. "Her mother was a truck driver in Afghanistan. That's why I assigned her to your daughter. She knows what your daughter is going through."

Lauren suddenly realized that nothing about this program was haphazard. Although it seemed relaxed, everything they did had a purpose. "Aren't parents supposed to drop their kids and get out of Dodge?"

"That's the plan, but we make exceptions when necessary. We try not to be rigid. Have you had lunch?" Before she could answer, he was guiding her away from the car and across the yard to the house when she heard a very loud, very plaintive noise.

"That must be the burro," she said as she looked toward the corral. "You can't forget that bray."

"Mistake," he said, following her gaze.

"Mistake?" she asked, puzzled.

"That's his name. It fits him and reminds me not to repeat that particular error of adopting a burro. He's loud and obnoxious and a troublemaker. He'll kick one of the mustangs, hide behind another, then bray about it."

"You didn't have to take him," she said logically.

"The mustangs were part of his herd, his family. He'd be lost without them. No one else would take him."

She stared at him. "You're a real softy masquerading as a tough guy."

"Don't let the ranch hands hear that."

"I suspect they know. How many employees do you have?"

"There's the cook, Betty Baker, and her husband, Ben, who is the fix-it guy around the house and stable. They live in a house on the ranch. There's Sandra, who is the bookkeeper and computer guru. She lives in town. Chet Hunter is my foreman. He and his wife, Ann, have a house over the hill.

"Then," he added, "there's the stable crew that takes care of the horses and the cowhands that look after our cattle. The last two are sort of interchangeable—they can do both jobs. Depends on what's needed at any particular time. They have to make sure the horses and cattle have water and grass and that the calves don't wander away in the unfenced areas. There's a lot of predators around here.

"The married employees live in town," he continued. "It's about a fifteen-minute drive. The single guys mostly use the bunkhouse where the boys will stay. They have to pledge to behave themselves during this month or move to town. The single women have quarters on the other end of the house."

"I'm impressed," she said.

"Don't be. Every year is a financial struggle."

"But you still do the program?"

"It's not that costly. All the outside professionals donate their services. We have the space available. My guys—and that includes the females—love doing it, although it's more work. I buy the mustangs cheap and can usually sell them for good prices after they're trained."

He saw her look back toward the barn. Despite his attempts to distract her, she was worrying. "She really is safe," he said.

She nodded. "She's had a horrific year and a half. There's good news, though. There was movement in her toes. That means she can have an almost normal walk."

"That *is* good news."

"And you were right. She fell in love with Leo when we arrived."

"Everyone does, and he's a diplomat. He spreads himself around this month. He's my dog the rest of the year."

"I'm going to get Julie a dog as soon as we get back to San Antonio. She's always wanted one, but pet ownership doesn't work well in the air force."

"Want advice?"

"Sure."

"Adopt a rescue," he said. "Leo's one. They're so appreciative of finding a home they do their best to please and they love fiercely. He's probably with the kids in the stable now. He relishes the role of greeter and comforter during this month."

"Like your mustangs?"

"I'm not sure whether they're appreciative or not," he said. "They would probably be happier roaming the West with their kind. Unfortunately, the government has other plans for them."

"After talking to you, I've been reading about it," she said.

"And did you reach any conclusion?"

"It's sad. Do you think that once gentled they ever think about the old, free days?"

"They have memory. They remember people. Places. They hold grudges against someone who harms them or one of theirs. But they also remember people who are good to them. One of the kids who came here three years ago returned last year to see the mare he rode, and she was ecstatic."

She studied him. He looked more civilized than he did three weeks ago, and was even more striking. His dark hair was shorter and neatly combed although a shock of hair still fell down on his forehead, and his tanned face was cleanly shaved. He still wore jeans but they were clean today, as were his boots. She also recognized the jean jacket but it, too, had obviously undergone rehabilitation. He would never be called handsome but he was certainly memorable in a sexy way.

He paused. "We'll take good care of her. Either Sally or I will keep in touch and tell you about her day. And, of course, Julie can call you anytime." He paused, then asked, "So, where in Covenant Falls are you staying? Let me guess…the Camel Trail Inn?"

She nodded.

"Good. You'll like it. I stay there when I take horses down there. Take the gold mine Jeep trip with Herman. It's hair-raising but you'll learn a lot about the history of the area.

"And," he added, "there's Parents' Day next Sunday. We'll have a barbecue out here, and you can see what they've accomplished." He reached up and touched her cheek and she realized a tear had rolled down.

"I'm fine."

"I'm sure you are."

She looked up at him. "How are your mustangs?"

"Getting used to fences. They're about ready for their sirens."

She raised an eyebrow. "The mystical sirens of literature? Didn't they lure people to their doom?"

He looked abashed for a moment. "Well, these are good sirens."

They reached the kitchen. He held the door open for her as she entered. As before, it smelled wonderful. It smelled aromatic. She could detect three different spices.

Betty greeted her as if she was her long-lost friend. "Mrs. MacInnes, it's grand to see you."

"Since she's a latecomer," Reese said, "maybe we can get her something to eat before she leaves. The rockslide trapped someone else again. I doubt they'll ever clear it. Her daughter can probably use a ham and cheese sandwich at the stables."

"I'll take it over while you two eat," Betty said as she ladled steaming soup into two large bowls, poured lemonade into two glasses and tucked two large pieces of homemade bread into the oven. "I noticed you didn't eat at the picnic," she scolded Reese. "So you eat something, too. The bread will be ready in a jiff."

"Yes, ma'am," he answered, and Lauren had to smile. The big, tough mustang tamer sounded like a chastened schoolboy.

Betty quickly made a fat sandwich, poured more lemonade into a paper cup, took the now-hot bread from the oven and placed a large slab of butter on a plate. She then whirled out the door with the sandwich and lemonade for Julie.

The whole process took place in the wink of an eye. "Did she really do that?" Lauren asked.

"Yep. I often tell her she missed out on a career in time management. The best thing is everything is good. She's an artist with seasoning. She's been with us twenty years. Met her husband while working here. He's as good at fixing stuff as she is at cooking."

The soup was not only good, it was exquisite. Lauren was hungry and ate rapidly. Then she looked up. His dark eyes were on her and he was smiling. Then their gazes met and a lightning bolt of heat ran through her.

Emotions tumbled around inside. Anxiety. Indecision. Guilt. And, worse, need that ran deep and strong. *How could she even think of another man?*

Dane had been the first and only man she'd ever loved. They'd had everything in common. Drive. Commitment. Love of flying. The air force and then their daughter. In the months since he died, she'd never had the slightest attraction to any man. She didn't think it was possible.

Now she was flooded with it. A warm glow started to puddle deep inside and the heat was spreading throughout her limbs. He'd made an impact when she first saw him in clothes that looked to have years of hard wear, muddy boots and a face badly in need of a shave. He'd looked as if he just stepped out of a hard-as-nails Western movie. She hadn't been sure she wanted him anywhere near her child.

In the short time she was with him, she'd discovered he was anything but hard as nails. There was an uncommon gentleness deep inside. It was in the way he talked about his kids, his mustangs, his staff, even his noisy new burro. She knew now why Patti adored him and wanted Julie to come here. If anyone could break through her daughter's walls, it was Reese and his people and animals.

The big question was how he remained single, which he apparently was, since he talked about nearly everyone on the ranch and nothing about a wife. Maybe estranged or divorced. In any event it wasn't her business.

He gave her a crooked smile as if he read her mind. She stood and he followed. "I should get on," she said. "Thank you for lunch." Her voice sounded stiff, even to her.

"You'll like Covenant Falls," he said, his gaze penetrating. "The history is striking. It's one of the oldest communities in Colorado. It has a great little museum."

He paused. "You might even want to go horseback riding. Try that bronc instead of a plane. Call Luke Daniels. Tell him I sent you. He and his wife teach horsemanship. They're the best teachers around."

Lauren led the way out. He touched the small of her back as they went outside and she felt electricity flow from his hand through her body. The warmth turned to fire as they reached her car and she turned around.

"We'll take good care of your daughter," he said.

"I know, but still…she's so fragile."

"I think she's a lot stronger than you think," he said as he opened the car door for her. She hesitated for a moment, then, her mind completely muddled, she stepped inside and drove off.

Chapter 6

The warmth of Reese's touch stayed with Lauren as she headed toward Covenant Falls.

Any number of feelings battered her as she headed east. She still wasn't sure about leaving her daughter to strangers, although that was tempered today when she saw the caring organization. She'd liked Robin and thought she would be good for her daughter.

As for herself, she couldn't remember when she'd last had a block of empty time. It should be exhilarating. It wasn't.

Since she always needed a goal, or mission, she decided to look for interesting places to take Julie after the month was over. They could have some adventures together. Maybe then she could narrow the distance between them.

Lauren thought she might even take Reese's suggestion about horseback riding lessons while staying at the inn. It would be something she could share with her daughter. She'd mentally filed the instructor's name Reese had given her.

She also had to consider her future. They would need a steady income soon. She didn't want to touch the insurance money. That was for Julie's education. Problem was there was nothing she wanted to do but fly. Nothing else she was qualified for. Now she faced weeks of inactivity while Julie was at the ranch.

She turned her full attention to the road ahead. The drive east was more pleasant than she'd hoped. It was winding, but well paved with little traffic, and it was beautiful country with towering pine trees lining fast-running streams. Julie would love it.

She was two-thirds of the way when she spotted a dirt road running to the left. On the side of the road was a sign that said Flying Lessons Available. It looked old and weathered. She wondered if it was still active. She stored it in the back of her brain.

Lauren knew she was trying to think of anything but Reese Howard. He kept intruding. It was unsettling. She had, in fact, been unsettled since the moment she'd met him three weeks ago. *Gobsmacked* was really the word, or nonword. She'd heard it someplace, and it seemed to fit now.

She'd been attracted to him from the moment they met. That had never happened before. It had taken Dane and herself a year before they even liked each other. They had been fierce competitors in flight school and advanced training.

He was from a wealthy family in the East and had all the manners of one. She was raised by a single mother who worked two jobs and still had difficulty paying for a new pair of cheap shoes. She found out later she was the lucky one. She had love and lots of it from her mother.

He hadn't. One night they were out with a group of pilots in San Antonio, and someone asked about his family. He said he didn't have one. The way he said it, though, struck a chord in her. And later, after several drinks, he let down his guard and she fell in love...

It had been a good marriage. He had a dry humor and cool professionalism as a pilot and was a friend as well as a colleague and husband. Most of all, she missed the way he'd loved her and their daughter. Because of his own background, he loved fiercely.

She hadn't thought she could care for anyone again. It hurt too much. Even though she and Dane shared a risky occupation, she had a hard time accepting the fact that he died at the hands of a drunk driver. There was something terribly ironic about that.

She'd been in a zombie emotional state since his death. It was Julie's needs that kept her going, but she knew she wasn't really living. She'd merely been surviving. Until now. Part of her resented it.

But there was something about Reese Howard, his mustangs, a dog named Leo and a braying burro that was reviving her. It was much too fast, though. She didn't know anything about him or whether there was someone special in his life.

She neared Covenant Falls and noticed a sign advertising the Camel Trail Inn two miles ahead. She followed Sally's directions and quickly found it. The town looked like a typical small one. She passed a Methodist church with a steeple, a lake fronted by small neat cottages on one side and picnic grounds and a beach on another.

Then she found the Camel Trail Inn. She hadn't expected much in a small town. The seediest motels are often called inns. But she was favorably impressed when she reached a wood-shingled, single-floor sprawling building. It was nearing 6:00 p.m. and she wondered what her daughter was doing. Hopefully, she was enjoying the picnic and show.

She parked in the half-filled parking lot and walked inside. The lobby was warm and welcoming with a large painting of a waterfall on one side, a huge rock fireplace on another, and a painting of the mountains on the wall in back of the front desk.

She approached the front desk, and a young man greeted her.

"I have a reservation," she said. "Lauren MacInnes."

"Oh, yes, we've been expecting you. Your room is ready." He smiled. "I'm Jimmy, assistant manager. If I can see your credit or debit card?" He made a quick copy of it and asked her to sign a card. Then he handed her three envelopes with her name on it.

She stared at them. "For me?"

"Seems you're popular around here," he said with a smile. "The one on the top is from the mayor."

He handed her a metal key. "Room 210, right around the corner on left. You have a great view of our mountain. There's complimentary wine and snacks every day from 4:00 p.m. to 7:00 p.m. in the library. It's just beyond the lobby on your right. Complimentary coffee and pastries are in the lobby at 6:00 a.m. and earlier if you're leaving before that hour. Just let us know."

"I'm impressed," she said. "Anything else?"

"Well, yes. We have two restaurants that deliver here. The menus and phone numbers are in your room. Maude's offers great Western cooking and the Rusty

Nail specializes in hamburgers and steaks. Both are veteran friendly. That's it, except we hope you enjoy your stay."

She was more than impressed. She only hoped the room was as pleasant.

She stopped first, though, at the library. Bottles of both white and red wine were available on a counter along with a tray of crackers, cheeses, slices of ham and raw veggies. She poured some red into the glass as she glanced through the shelves full of books. Many were Western and Colorado history but there was also a novel section. "All donated books are appreciated," said a sign, "and fiction books can be adopted."

She liked the sign. She found a novel, tucked it under her arm and, carrying the glass of wine, found her room and went inside. Her suitcase was still in the car, but she looked out the window at the mountain overshadowing the town and sipped the wine. The luggage in the car could wait.

She opened the envelope from the mayor. It was an invitation to dinner Tuesday night at her home. The second letter contained an invitation to "join the veterans of Covenant Falls for its weekly poker game" tomorrow at the city library and museum. The third was an invitation from Andrea Stuart, Chamber of Commerce President, to visit the city museum and library.

Did they do this for every guest? Or had someone arranged it? Someone from Eagles' Roost. Whatever, she did feel welcome and not just as a hotel guest. She particularly liked the poker game invitation. It had been a long time since she'd joined in a military poker game. It would feel like old times. Good times. She looked up at a horseshoe over the door. Good luck. She needed some.

She went out for her suitcase. She always packed light, again a legacy from her air force days. Then she returned to her room. She looked at the mayor's invitation, then the clock. It was seven-thirty. Did she really want to spend Tuesday evening at the home of someone she didn't know, and a mayor's home at that?

It was an informal note signed by Eve Manning. Curiosity won. *Why not?*

She called the number. A woman answered.

"Mayor Manning?" she asked.

"Eve," the woman corrected. "You must be Major MacInnes?"

"Yes, but it's just Lauren. I'm not in the air force now."

"You've come to the right place. This town is full of veterans. The police chief is a former army chopper pilot, a former SEAL runs a Horses for Heroes program, a former battlefield nurse runs our Chamber of Commerce and operates the library/museum. I don't think you want me to go on, but that's just the beginning."

"No service rivalry?"

"I can't say that, but it's good-natured. Anyway, welcome. My husband will pick you up at 6:30 p.m. Tuesday if that's okay. I have to warn you first, though. My house is a zoo."

"I like zoos," Lauren said. She paused, then asked, "On the way down here, I saw a sign advertising flying lessons. It looked old. Do you know if it's still in business?"

"Sure. That's Otis Davies. He's in his late seventies, and is as sharp as people half his age. He sometimes flies feed into Reese's ranch if the roads are iced over, and he does some teaching. He used to be air force, too, served in Vietnam. He'd be overjoyed with a visit from a fellow pilot."

"I'll do that. I'll see you Tuesday," she said.

"I hope you enjoy your stay. Reese is a good friend of my husband, Josh, and myself, and he said you were staying here as long as a week. Reese said we had a lot in common, and I look forward to meeting you. You and Josh can argue the merits of air force over army."

In just those few seconds, she knew she would like Eve Manning. She accepted, then asked, "Will he be at the poker game tomorrow night?"

"Pretty sure he will. I'm envious every time he leaves, but the rule is absolute. Veterans only. I understand that good-natured arguments are the norm."

"You talked me into it. Should I call them?"

"No. Just show up. I really hope you're good. My husband is getting a little too cocky. How do you like the inn?"

"It seems too good to be true."

"We have a great innkeeper. She just married one of the vets you'll meet tomorrow night. But now I'm afraid I'm confusing you. The story is we've been flooded by vets here, most of them in the past five years."

Maybe she could find out more about Reese then.

"You must be tired," Eve said. "I'll let you go. I look forward to meeting you in person Tuesday."

"Sounds good."

"Good night and don't worry about your daughter. Reese is great at what he does. He can look tough, but he's a gentle soul inside. Just don't tell him I said that," Eve added before she hung up.

Lauren thought about the last words as she took an-other sip of wine and considered getting a refill if there was any left. Gentle soul was the right way to describe him, when she considered the burro, his recommendation about dog adoption and the way he discussed the plight of mustangs. It was just packaged in a gruff exterior.

She wondered why he wasn't married, or maybe he was and his wife was somewhere else. Patti had never mentioned his marital status, but then she'd never asked.

It was none of her business. She would get that second glass of wine, take a hot bath in the large bathtub and read the book she'd selected from the inn's library.

She soon discovered it wasn't that easy. She simply couldn't get the tall, self-assured rancher out of her head, no matter how hard she tried. There was so much she didn't know. And now she wondered. Why was he looking after other people's children rather than his own? He certainly seemed to have everything going for him.

She'd known loners in the service. And she would swear he wasn't one. He'd been too easy with her and she'd noticed the camaraderie between him and his crew. And yet, there was a reserve about him, even as he discussed a topic important to him.

He and Eve's husband were apparently good friends. Maybe, just maybe, she could coax some more information about him. And then, the question was, why did she care?

After Lauren drove away, Reese took the teens to the stable to pick their horses for the duration of the program. He'd selected eight of the best-behaved horses for the kids to choose from. They were all ranch horses, accustomed to different riders. He'd trained most of them himself and knew their temperaments.

He and Chet led them out into the ring, and the kids wandered among them until a connection was made. The buddies helped, telling his or her partner about each of the horses, but it was really a matter of chemistry: a horse reaching over to nuzzle a hand, a friendly whinny, a nod of the head.

Reese was pleased to note that each of the four found their horse relatively quickly.

Reese paid particular attention to Julie. She hung back at first but then a white horse nudged her. She tentatively gave Snowflake half of a carrot each carried out with them. The horse took it gingerly, chomped it down, then nudged Julie for another. She seemed to grin at Julie and put her head on her shoulder as if to say "You're mine." Julie gave her the rest of the carrot.

"She's the infamous Snowflake, the curse of every cowman on the ranch," Robin said fondly. "Just because of her name. Tells you something about cowboys, doesn't it?" She grinned. "They're a superstitious bunch."

"You, too?" Julie asked.

"No, I escaped that particular affliction."

"Well, I think she's been maligned," Julie said. "I'll take her if that's okay."

"Good for you," Reese said, and Julie spun around. She was a pretty girl with auburn hair rather than her mother's fiery color. "She probably has the smoothest gait of any of the others."

Julie looked nonplussed. "I didn't know you were there?"

"I was wondering who would pick Snowflake. You have a good eye."

"Can we mount today?" Julie asked. There was eagerness in her voice now.

"No, there's not time," he said. "And the hands are all getting ready for a cookout and variety show tonight. It's a great way to get to know them. Anytime you have a question, just ask them, although I think Robin knows as much about this ranch as anyone does. Did she tell you that she came here as one of you three years ago?"

Julie nodded.

"I have to get back to the house," he said, "but stay and talk to Snowflake for a while."

"What do I say?"

"Anything you want to," he said. "I guarantee she doesn't gossip."

She gave him that "how lame can you get?" look, but then smiled. It was blinding. She was her mother's daughter. His nephew had better look out.

He left on that note. The kids would spend the next hour getting to know their horses. Talk to him or her. Brush them. Generally spoil them. Their buddy would be with them, telling them a little about the horse, what he liked or didn't like. Mounting would come tomorrow. There were too many emotions today. Excitement. Fear. Uncertainty. Horses sensed emotions and reacted to them.

In a week they would feel secure on the horse's back; in the second week they would learn tricks together; in the third they would race the other riders and in the last week their hearts would hurt when they were separated but they would be stronger for it.

In the meantime, there was the cookout in the large picnic area at the back of the house. The menu included grilled hot dogs and hamburgers, corn on the cob, chili, baked beans, coleslaw and a choice of desserts.

As they ate dessert after, the variety show started.

The ice was broken almost immediately as it started with cowboy humor, which included skits and corny jokes. One ranch hand had taught his horse dancing steps.

Rope tricks came next, and the kids were invited to try it. His nephew, Nathan, ended the program by playing the guitar and singing cowboy songs, urging all to join in on the more well-known ones. By then, the kids were usually full, sleepy and happy.

He wished Lauren MacInnes—all the parents—could see their teens. But especially Lauren. That thought worried him. He was content now, and it had taken him many years to get here. He didn't need someone to upset the world he'd helped build. Yet, he couldn't get her face, especially those expressive eyes, out of his head.

Her daughter did well today. She apparently had the same grit as her mother. After a first hesitation, she chose a good horse, listened intently to the instructions and did her best to follow them.

After everyone dispersed from the cookout, Reese went to the stable and saddled his favorite horse, Max. Chet met him as he walked Max out.

"That went well," Chet said.

"Yeah. Seems that way. We have a good bunch of people here."

"Best crew I've worked with," Chet said. "That's because of you."

Reese shook his head. "You're the foreman."

"Going for a ride?" Chet asked.

"I'm just going to the Roost. Think for a while."

"About anything in particular? Like a certain woman?"

"When did you become a detective?"

"It wasn't hard, my friend. I watched you with her.

You were…intense with each other. Both times. Three weeks ago, and again today."

"That's absurd," Reese said. "I admit she's an attractive woman, but…she has a career of her own. She would never be happy here even if I was interested."

"Like Cara?"

"Yeah."

"Two different people," Chet said. "You know I was worried about my Ann when we married. She was a city girl. Turned out she was a cowgirl at heart. She loves it here. Something tells me Mrs. MacInnes might have a bit of an adventurer in her, too."

"I hardly know her," Reese said. "And what in the hell would a pilot do here in the middle of nowhere?"

"You never know," Chet said, "unless you give it a try."

"Don't you have something else to do?"

"Not at the moment."

"Go find something," Reese said in mock irritation.

"Yes, sir," Chet said with a grin and left.

Reese rode out. There was a near full moon tonight and a million stars and he could find his way easily. He was used to riding at night. There'd been stormy nights when he and the hands were out soothing frightened cattle to keep them from smashing through fences as lightning flashed around them.

The ranch was located in a valley bordered on three sides by peaks, one of which harbored eagles. They'd roosted on the ledge of one of the peaks since the first Howard arrived. Henry Howard had been a trapper and mountain man when he followed an eagle into the valley. He never had the desire to leave. The game and fish were plentiful, the gazing great for cattle, and there was plenty of fresh water from the mountains.

Reese dismounted, and Max drank from a spring next to a fenced-off area. Reese opened a gate and squatted in front of his father's marker. He'd both loved and feared his father as a boy and pitied him years later as he wasted away.

The family cemetery was located here, according to family lore, because it was an eagle that guided Henry to this place. The souls of the family members could look up and watch the eagles soar. There were twenty-three headstones. Four of the family were returned from overseas: one died in World War I, two in France during World War II and one in Vietnam. The others ranged from 1882 to 2010. The most recent one contained no remains, only what could have been.

He knelt before it for a moment, then mounted and rode home.

Chapter 7

The poker game was all that Eve said it would be.

Lauren had spent the morning exploring the area. Covenant Falls was the most amazingly friendly town she'd ever visited. Almost everyone she met was a veteran or related to one. The first lunch at Maude's Diner was free for veterans. And the steak was good.

She met and immediately liked Andrea Stuart, an injured former battlefield nurse who organized the town museum. The museum was one place she really wanted Julie to visit, not only because the history was exciting but also to see how well Andrea dealt with a major injury.

Lauren also studied the information sheet on things to do in Covenant Falls. In addition to visiting the museum and falls, it listed the Jeep trip Reese had mentioned and horseback riding.

She was going to be here a week. Why not try it? Reese had told her about Luke Daniels. The phone number was included on the information sheet.

She called and made an appointment for a riding lesson for the next day. When she mentioned Reese's name, it was readily made. He was obviously a hero around here...

Thirteen people, including three women, came to the museum's community room for the penny poker game. All armed services and ages were included. There was beer and food and kidding and she felt very much at home.

She owed Reese for mentioning it and, apparently, for the invitation. Or perhaps he'd just wanted her not to worry about her daughter. Anyway, it was much too late to call him when the game disbanded at 10:00 p.m.

When she reached the inn, it was ten thirty. There had been no call from Julie on either her cell phone or room phone. A positive sign. She undressed and stepped into a hot bath with a book. Just as she sank into the bubbles thoughtfully provided by the inn, the room phone rang.

There was an extension in the bathroom. She stood up, grabbed it and settled back inside the bathtub.

"Mrs. MacInnes?" There was no mistaking the deep Western drawl when she answered.

"Yes?" Her voice was harsher than she intended because she worried the call indicated trouble.

"Sorry to call so late, but I was pretty sure you wouldn't be back at the inn much before now since Monday is poker night. You expressed some interest, so I called the other parents first." He paused. "Just wanted you to know that Julie had a good day. She picked out Snowflake yesterday, saddled her this morning and with the help of some steps we have, was able to mount on her own. She rode around the ring with no problems, even a slow trot."

"I wish I had been there," she said with mist beginning to blind her.

"I get that. How do you like Covenant Falls?"

"I know now why your sister suggested it. It's great. I did go to the poker game tonight and they accused me of being a ringer."

"You won?"

"Second place. I went home with seven whole dollars."

"I'm impressed. I played with them once and lost everything I had."

"All of three or four dollars, I suspect." She hesitated, then asked what she'd been waiting for all day. "Tell me more about Julie. How is she with the other kids?"

"Good. They seem friendly. Today they've been mostly involved with horses. They're beginning to understand how much work it takes to own one. They had dinner, compared notes and headed for bed."

"She really enjoyed riding?" Lauren needed confirmation.

"If a broad smile is any indication, I can confirm it," he said.

She blinked back a tear. "Thanks for calling."

"It's a ritual at the end of the first full day. I do it with all the parents."

She wasn't sure how to read that, but it didn't really matter. She was too pleased with the news. "How was the variety show last night?"

"You'll have to ask Julie about that, but I think I saw a few smiles. Despite what I said, the show was pretty good but then I'm prejudiced. There are a few really talented people in the group. And some real hams."

"But that's what makes it fun, right?"

"Right," he replied.

"I'm following your suggestion," she said. "I'm going to take some riding lessons starting tomorrow."

"With Luke Daniels?"

"Yep. Along with your suggestion, his number was included in the inn's recommendations."

"Good. He and his wife are good teachers. His wife will be up here for the last two weeks of the program," he said, then added, "I'll see you Sunday. I'm sure your daughter's going to want to show you some good equine moves."

"I'm going to dinner at the Mannings' ranch tomorrow night. Someone seems to have informed everyone in town that I've arrived."

There was a silence, then, "Did I overstep?"

"Nope, I like being the toast of Covenant Falls, including a free lunch at Maude's and being the honored guest at the Famous Covenant Falls Veteran All-Star Penny Poker Game. Haven't tried the other eatery yet, but something tells me there's a free beer or something there for me." She paused, then added, "They seem to know you well." It was a question more than a statement.

She could almost see him shrug. "Not that well. When I heard about the Horses for Heroes program and that they were looking to borrow trained horses, I offered to loan them several of mine. I get as much out of it as they do. Even sold some of the horses for a nice profit." There was something in his voice that tugged at her.

It was as if he was ashamed of doing something worthy.

He was a very complicated man despite her first impression. The first time they met, she saw raw masculine strength. It seemed he cared little what other people thought. Tough. Self-contained. She hadn't been sure at all that she wanted to leave her daughter in his care.

Sunday, though, she'd noticed how he treated all his employees. It was as if each one, even the newest hand, was a treasured family member. *Because he didn't have much of his own?*

As far as she knew he had his sister and her son and, on the edges, some distant relatives like Patti.

But it was none of her business. None at all.

"When you come next Sunday," Reese said, "I'll select a horse for you and show you more of the ranch."

"I hope you know I've never been near a horse, much less atop one." She changed the subject. "I'm confused about who's who in Covenant Falls. I keep running into more and more veterans, and they all seem to know me."

"Same thing happened to me the first time I visited," he said. "If I were the least bit competent with a computer, I would send you a Covenant Falls residents' graph." She could almost see his rueful smile as he said it

"Without Sandra—I don't think you met her but she's our accountant and business manager—we would be in trouble. My computer skills are nil, probably because I resent modern technology. Kids can't add two plus two these days without looking at a computer."

She laughed. "I'm pretty good with computers," she admitted. "You have to be these days if you fly modern aircraft. But I would be terrible with a bunch of mustangs."

"I'm not so sure about that," he said. "But I'm keeping

you away from whatever you were doing. I just wanted to tell you Julie's doing fine. I have one more family to call."

Lauren thought they were both conscious of a certain intimacy that crept into the conversation and they were trying to avoid it. Their lives were going in opposite directions. He was probably a confirmed bachelor since apparently he hadn't been married for a long time. At least that was what she'd pieced together. And she still mourned her husband and had a daughter who was still fragile.

"Thanks," she said and hung up before they lingered longer, except she wanted to linger. She'd discovered new things about him while she was in Covenant Falls, and he was even more of an enigma. She slipped deeper into the bathwater and turned on the hot water again, not that she needed any more heat. How could a voice create such a warm reaction in her? It was deep and sexy and made her toes curl.

Then she immediately felt guilty. Was she being untrue to Dane?

She finished her bath and it was nearly eleven thirty. All in all, it was a good day. Much better than she expected. She'd been instantly accepted, and she hadn't realized how much she needed adult company. She was beginning to feel like a real person again.

She was excited the next morning. Her riding lesson was at eleven. It was a challenge and she badly needed one.

After a coffee and two cinnamon rolls, she headed for the Covenant Falls General Store where she purchased riding boots, riding pants and several shirts. She knew exactly what to buy because she had bought them for Julie.

She liked Luke immediately. He was probably in his seventies but he looked younger and his energy was contagious. He didn't start her in the saddle, but led her through the steps of saddling the mare he'd chosen and explained the best way to approach a horse.

Once she was in the saddle and the stirrups adjusted, he instructed her on her seat and the correct way of holding the reins. Then he instructed her to walk around the ring. She was stiff and uncomfortable, worried that she would prove to be an inept pupil, but after a few moments Luke put her at ease, assuring her that every new rider felt the same.

After walking around the ring several times, Luke coaxed her into trying a slow trot. At first, Lauren felt as if she was going down while the horse went up, but then Luke's quiet instruction relaxed her enough that she and the horse went in the same vertical direction.

Exhilaration ran through her for the first time since she'd left the air force. By the end of the lesson, she'd successfully trotted around the ring and yearned for more.

In just those minutes she started to understand Reese's passion. There was a sense of freedom, much like she felt piloting a plane, only it was more…personal. She liked feeling the power of the horse and the way it felt when they moved together. The hour stretched into two.

"You're going to be sore as hell tomorrow," he said as he ended the lesson and showed her how to cool the horse down. "I suggest a hot bath tonight."

She made an appointment for a lesson the next day, then she hurried home to take a hot bath as instructed before having dinner with the Mannings. She decided to skip lunch since it was already midafternoon.

Cleansed of horse, she was waiting at the inn entrance when Eve's husband, Josh Manning, arrived. She'd met him and his former military dog, Amos, at the poker game and liked him immediately. He reminded her of Reese.

"I heard you went riding today," he said when she settled in the front passenger seat. Amos was taking the entire backseat.

"Of course you did," she replied. "I heard about the grapevine. No wonder there's no crime in Covenant Falls. It would be all over town in five seconds—the who, what, when and why."

He smiled. "True. It drove me crazy when I first arrived. Now I'm used to it."

When she arrived at the Manning house, she was met by a boy of twelve or so. "This is Nick," Josh said, "and he is a keeper of the zoo we have here. He's been minding the grill for me."

It was altogether a very good evening. She liked Eve immensely, especially when she heard the story of the couple's first meeting. When Josh appeared in Covenant Falls, he was apparently the terror of the town. He was angry at the world and showed it. Eve defied the town to defend his right to be angry.

She was still mayor, and now he was half owner of the Camel Trail Inn among several other businesses. The evening went fast, with great steaks grilled outside and tales about Covenant Falls. After the food was devoured, she was introduced to Nick's dogs. In addition to Amos, she counted five, all rescues of varying sizes, and Dizzy the cat, who ran in circles when meeting her. There were also two horses, Beauty and the Beast.

The conversation turned to the riding lesson. "How did you like it?" Eve asked.

"I liked it far better than I thought I would. It always seemed like a slow form of transportation."

Eve laughed. "A lot more personal, though."

"That's true and I have aches to prove it."

"Take a long hot bath tonight," Eve advised.

"I did that earlier and I'm still beginning to feel aches in muscles I never knew I had."

"They'll fade quickly," Josh said. "I know."

They were on the way home when he asked, "Are you returning to San Antonio?"

"I'm not sure. I don't think so. Too many reminders."

"Think about us. It's a great community. We have a good school, winter sports, even a summer pageant."

They reached the inn. "I have to make a living," Lauren said. I'm not sure I can find one around here although I'm beginning to really like Colorado."

He started to get out of the car and she shook her head. "I'm fine," she said. "Thanks for the evening. Thanks for making me feel so welcome."

He grinned. "Tell Reese hello for me. He's one hell of a good guy."

She was getting into bed thirty minutes later when she received a call from her daughter. There was a note of excitement in it. "Snowflake is wonderful." Her voice was bubbly for the first time since the accident. "Maybe we can get a horse?" she asked tentatively.

"I thought you weren't supposed to call until the third day," Lauren said before answering the question. She needed time to think.

"This is Tuesday," Julie said. "Sunday, Monday, Tuesday. See. Three days."

"I don't think they meant to call Sunday the first day."

"But it *was*," Julie insisted. "And I wanted to tell you about Snowflake."

"And I'm happy you did," she said. "I liked Snowflake, too."

"Then maybe we can get one…"

Lauren was a lot more receptive to the idea of a horse than she would have been before her lesson. She didn't mention that. She didn't want to spoil her daughter's excitement by barging in. "You know it's not as easy to buy a horse as a dog. We can think about it, though," she said.

"I cantered today." Her daughter exploded with excitement. "The instructor said I had a natural seat." Lauren's heart skipped a beat. Julie sounded every bit as excited as when she'd won an important race.

"That's terrific," she replied.

"Well, goodbye," Julie said. "I just wanted you to know about Snowflake."

"Goodbye, sweetie. I can't wait to see you ride."

After hanging up, the past three days passed through Lauren's mind in a flash.

Maybe she'd been wrong not to have ventured out sooner but then she'd not had much opportunity. Yet, Bob and other fellow pilots had invited her to parties and games. She'd always used Julie as an excuse to say no. She hadn't felt that she should have fun when Dane was gone.

The poker game had helped alleviate the sense of emptiness when she left Eagles' Roost alone. The following day's riding lesson had helped even more. The subsequent supper at the Mannings' ranch produced one of the best steaks she'd ever had. It was a fun evening, one of the first since Dane's death, and she fell in love with Josh's former military dog. It made her even more determined to find one for Julie as soon as they settled somewhere permanently.

But where would that be? She'd planned on San Antonio but the proximity to the air base would be a constant temptation to rejoin. She liked Colorado but where could she make a living? What was she trained for? Nothing but flying.

Maybe she would go online and explore opportunities in the area. She refused to question why Colorado instead of Texas. After all, it was just an exercise, an exploration. Something to do.

She refused to consider that a tall Colorado rancher might have something to do with it, even as he haunted her thoughts.

Wednesday morning was free. She had her second riding lesson at three. Problem was what to do this morning, and then what to do for the next three weeks. Except for the horseback riding, she was running short of things to do in Covenant Falls. Maybe she would check out the flying school she'd noticed on the drive to Covenant Falls.

She'd promised her daughter she wouldn't fly again. But that was military flying. A short flight on a small plane didn't count.

But then that was supposing that a plane was available. Besides, she really just wanted to talk flying. She drove to the sign she'd found days ago, turned and drove another mile until she came to a rickety sprawling building with a two-seater anchored outside. She parked next to an elderly Ford and knocked at the metal door of the building before trying it and finding it open. It reminded her of the time twenty-two years earlier when she'd visited another flyer in a similar building.

A gray-haired man was working on a cargo plane. He turned. And studied her. "You that pilot that's staying in Covenant Falls?"

"Guilty," she said. "How did you know?"

"No secrets in this area." He reached out his hand. "I'm Otis Davies, and you don't look like you need lessons."

She was grateful he didn't add "at your age." "You're air force?" he asked instead.

"*Was* air force," she said. "I had to resign when my daughter was injured."

"Can't stay away from a plane, huh?"

"Something like that."

"Going to be around here for a while?"

He was obviously a man of few words. "At least three weeks," she said, "and I'm not sure how long I'll be in the area after that."

"Too bad," he said. "I can use a pilot at times."

"Teaching?"

He shook his head. "Some. But mostly freight. We get a lot of desperate calls from ranchers who need feed or other supplies in a hurry, particularly when there's bad weather."

She shook her head, wondering why she had come here in the first place, why something inside propelled her here. "I'm afraid I won't be here long enough. Our home is in San Antonio, but thanks for the offer."

And her home *was* in Texas, despite her curiosity about this area. Her friends were there. Julie's friends were there. Heck, admit it, the base was there and all its temptation.

He nodded, accepting the answer. He looked at the plane he was working on. "Doesn't look like much, but it's in good shape. I also have a two-seater outside I use for teaching."

"Were you in the service?" she asked.

"Air force. End of 'Nam."

She saluted him and he returned it. "Anytime you want to go up, just let me know," he said.

"Thanks. I might take you up on that."

"Just give me a couple of hours' notice. I'll have her gassed up."

"The sign says flying lessons," she pointed out.

"Not much interest in learning from an old fossil," he replied. "Now, if a hotshot air force fighter pilot was on the faculty, I would fill up pretty darn fast."

"I was taught by an *old fossil*," she said with a grin. "He also went back to Vietnam era. Best pilot I ever knew. Knew more about flying, real flying, than a lot of people flying today. He got me into the Air Force Academy."

"What's his name?"

"Hank Douglas."

"Hell, I knew him. One of the best air commanders in 'Nam."

"I figured as much. I didn't know his rank, but I knew someone helped me get into the academy and I thought it might be him."

He eyed her with more interest. "I'm serious. There's more freight business and flight training to be had if I had the help," he added. "That's an offer, young lady."

"I'll remember that," she said.

The hunger to fly ate at her as she left and drove back to the inn. She'd wanted to sit in the cockpit even if it meant piloting a past-its-prime cargo plane or the two-seater training plane she saw. Her first experience in the sky was in a two-seater and she would never forget the awe she felt. She didn't think she would ever lose it. She would dearly love to awaken that love in young people.

She reached the inn in time to change for her riding lesson.

"How is your daughter?" Luke asked when she walked up to him at the stable.

"Excellent. I'm told she's a natural. I need to catch up."

"You're doing good, Mrs. MacInnes. Better than most."

"I want to be better than that," she said.

"That's what I like to hear," Luke replied.

An hour later she was cantering around the ring with more sureness.

"Don't get too confident," Luke said. "That's when you get in trouble."

"I won't," she replied. "That's one thing we're taught in flight school. Overconfidence kills."

"It's a good thing to remember."

When they finished, she requested an appointment for Tuesday of next week. She would definitely stay in Covenant Falls for at least the next three weeks.

Her daughter called that evening when Lauren was in the bathtub, bathing off horse, and easing muscle pain with inn-supplied bath salts.

"Hi, Mom," Julie said with a lilt in her voice Lauren hadn't heard in a year and a half.

"Julie, I'm so glad you called. You sound great." And she did. Her daughter's voice was filled with an enthusiasm she hadn't heard in way too long.

"Well, I'm good. Snowflake and I cantered today," she said, and Lauren heard the pride in her voice. "I love Snowflake," Julie continued. "She likes me, too. She nuzzles my cheek when I go to her stall."

"Is that healthy?"

"Mommmm…"

Lauren had heard that plaintive sound before. It translated into a "how can you be so lame?" moan.

She ignored it and, instead, asked, "What about the other kids?" hoping that Julie was making friends.

"I like them, particularly Jenny. She's shy but smart. She…lost her mother. We've been exchanging books."

"You have time to read books?"

"Not much. We have exercise classes in the morning. A shrink, Dr. Evans, was here last night. He just talked, wanted us to know he's available."

"What about your buddy, Robin?"

"She's kinda like the sister I always wanted," Julie said. "She said I would really like the trip up into the mountains during the last week."

"It sounds really good."

There was a silence, then Julie asked, "When are you coming back?"

"Sunday," Lauren said. "I understand there will be other moms and dads there, too."

A silence, then sadness entered her daughter's voice. "I wish Dad could see me on Snowflake."

"I do, too, sweetie," Lauren said. "He would be proud."

More silence. Pain shared. "I should go," Julie said.

"This is game night. We drew straws and I won so I get to choose it. Everyone has a week."

"What did you choose?"

"Scrabble."

"I should have known. You can crush them."

"Is that any way for a mom to talk?" her daughter asked.

Julie was sounding like the old Julie, the one before the accident. Lauren's heart swelled. What had happened in the past few days? Some kind of magic, undoubtedly. Horse magic, maybe. "Sorry about that," she said.

"My foot is better," Julie suddenly burst out. "I can move it a little."

"Why didn't you tell me that in the beginning?"

"It's just a little."

"A little is a big deal," Lauren said. "It means the transplant worked. It will get better now. I'm so happy for you, love."

"I should go now," Julie said.

"Love you, kiddo."

"I love you, too," her daughter said, and Lauren's heart sang.

Chapter 8

Today was Sunday!

Today she would return to Eagles' Roost. That was the only thing on her mind when Lauren woke as the first glimmer of light crept into her room. She couldn't still her eagerness to begin the day. She took a quick shower, dressed rapidly in running shorts and a green T-shirt and went for a short run before heading for the coffee and pastries in the inn's lobby.

The sky was overcast. *Please don't let it rain.*

She'd been waiting for today all week. Luke's schedule had been filled Thursday through Friday, but she'd booked time for next Tuesday and Wednesday. She'd spent the rest of the week doing touristy things. She'd gone to lunch with Eve and Stephanie Phillips, the town veterinarian, whom she liked immensely.

In truth, she liked everyone in Covenant Falls. Stephanie had given her some tips about dogs since Lauren definitely wanted one for Julie. It was first on her list when her daughter finished the program.

"I know of several rescues that would make excellent house pets," Stephanie had said. "Just let me know if you want to bring Julie over, and I'll have them at the office."

"Reese Howard suggested—no, make that emphatically suggested—a rescue," Lauren said. "And my daughter fell in love with his Leo."

Stephanie grinned. "He found Leo wandering on his ranch. Reese says the dog found the place he'd been looking for, just like the original Howard. I think it was love at first sight for both parties. Have you been on the Jeep trip yet?"

"No, but it's on my schedule for Saturday."

"Take a pillow. It's bumpy but a lot of fun."

Lauren didn't follow the advice and wished she had. It was definitely bumpy, but fun, and she planned to take Julie on it when she completed Junior Ranchers. Lauren had bounced all over the Jeep as their guide drove through rough terrain to see several broken-down shacks and some holes in the hills. But bearded Herman Mann was a storyteller of the first order and didn't stop regaling her with tales of the Colorado gold rush.

But as much as she'd enjoyed the past few days, she lived for Sunday at Eagles' Roost. The parents were invited from Sunday noon until six but now that she was knowledgeable about rockslides, gasoline truck leaks and other possible obstructions, Lauren decided to leave early. She certainly didn't want to be late again.

The inn lobby was more crowded than usual as guests checked out. Her reservation ran out today. When the desk clerk had a moment, she approached to prolong her stay.

She went back to her room and studied her limited wardrobe. She didn't want to be overdressed or underdressed. In the end she told herself she was being ridiculous and put on one of the new pairs of jeans she'd bought at the Covenant Falls General Store, along with a pullover shirt and her new pair of riding boots.

She took her time on the road, stopping several times at scenic spots where she took photos. Despite her dawdling, she arrived a little after ten-thirty. No rockslides or gas on the road.

When Lauren drove into the parking area, she saw her daughter in the riding ring along with Jenny. Julie was riding Snowflake. A woman in her thirties stood in the middle of the ring directing the girls.

Lauren parked and stepped out of the car. Not wanting to disturb the riders, she stood next to the car and watched as each rider went through an apparent routine: a walk, a trot, then a canter. Having been on horseback earlier that week, she recognized how smoothly the two handled their horses.

She was impressed. And proud. Her daughter sat straight and yet looked comfortable. Julie was intent on the instructor. Robin and two young teenage boys sat on the fence watching.

Then she saw Reese Howard and his foreman emerge from the stables, Leo by their sides. Reese said something to the foreman and they separated. He walked over to her. Leo reached her first and offered his paw even as his tail frantically wagged.

"I think he remembers you," Reese said.

"I think he does that to everyone," she said.

"Maybe, but not with as much enthusiasm." He studied her for a moment. "You're early," he noted with a smile.

"I thought it might be a positive change," she replied as a ripple of reaction ran through her. Had she imagined it or did he look even more appealing today? "And," she added, "it looked like rain in Covenant Falls. I didn't want to be late again."

His smile widened. "I'm glad you came early. The weather forecast here predicts rain tonight."

"Julie looks wonderful," she said. "She called the other night. I haven't heard that excitement in her voice since the accident."

"You said she was a natural athlete. You were right."

"She looks intent on what she's doing," she said. "Just as she used to be before a race. Who's the instructor?"

"Mary Abbot. She's an exceptional instructor. She's made training videos."

"You've made them, too, according to Patti," she said.

He shrugged. "The same company uses both of us, Mary for beginning riders and myself for training mustangs. We're just a few among many other horsemen."

"Can I find it?"

"Probably, if you look hard enough."

He obviously wasn't going to help. "Patti's proud of you."

"It goes two ways. She worked here several summers to earn money for school. I wanted to help, but she wants to do it on her own, and she's damned stubborn about it."

"What about your nephew?"

"He's also a good horseman. Sally brought him here when he was two. I put him on a horse when he was four, a year younger than when I started, but he wanted it. He kept wandering out to see the horses and I thought, hoped, he wanted the ranch in his future. But as much as he likes our horses, he likes music more, and he's damn good. Plays at clubs in this area, even did a stint in Denver."

"And you approve?"

"It's not up to me to approve or disapprove. He's seventeen and if I tried to force him into anything, he'd hate it."

Something in his tone told her there was experience in those words. As if he suddenly realized it, he shrugged. "He might change his mind. Sometimes reality hits. But he should have his chance."

"Did you have a choice?" she asked. "Patti said you had to take over when you were twenty."

His gaze bored into her. "Yes, I had a choice," he said bluntly. "I could have walked away. I chose not to."

But he couldn't walk away. She knew instinctively he was not a man to run away from responsibility even at a young age. "Have you ever regretted it?"

"Doesn't everyone have a moment of doubt about choices they made?" he asked.

There was a quiet intensity in the words that fascinated her. She'd heard it before when he talked about his mustangs, then again when he talked about his kids.

"No," she said. "I always wanted to fly."

"You had a hard decision when you left the air force," he said. "Do you regret that?" Their glances met. Held steady. Challenging.

"When you have a child, choices narrow," she said simply. "Julie's the most important person in my life, the most important everything."

He turned away, his attention going back to the riders in the ring, but not before she saw pain in his eyes.

"She really is good," Lauren said.

"Yes, she is," Reese said. "She knows it. Look at her expression. It's that athleticism you mentioned. She needed to exercise it."

The other girl, Jenny—a blonde a little heavier than Julie's slim form—was riding smoothly but not with Julie's grace. Jenny stopped at the direction of the woman in the center of the ring. She adjusted Jenny's hands on the reins and then the stirrups.

Julie turned then and saw Lauren and waved. Her face was alive again, her eyes shining. In one week she had her old daughter back, at least for today. Lauren knew it was only a beginning. Her daughter still had a long way to go. But there was spirit in that face again.

"She looks happy," she said. "It's the first time since the accident."

"That smile started a few days ago. Robin told me about it. I think it was the day she found her seat and trotted around the ring." He looked as proud of Julie as if she were his own daughter, and she thought he felt the same about the other three.

"When will they meet their mustangs?" she asked.

"Monday. They'll spend two hours a day with them twice a day, sometimes longer."

She wanted to see that. She really wanted to see it. "I took those riding lessons you suggested," she said.

"How does it compare to flying?" he asked.

She relaxed. "Doesn't quite have the highs, but I could easily become addicted."

He smiled at the pun. It crinkled the area around his eyes and even produced the smallest of dimples. She remembered that smile from the time he told her about the burro.

"I thought you might," he said. "Have you had anything to eat?"

"You ask that when you've stayed at the Camel Trail Inn?" she asked in return.

"I guess that answers my questions about whether you liked it. Their morning pastries is one reason I stay there when I'm in town rather than a friend's bunkhouse."

"Another week at the Camel Trail Inn, and I won't be able to get on a horse or in a cockpit."

"Are you going back to San Antonio after this?" he asked.

"For a few months anyway," she said. "I have a lease on a house, and Julie's doctors are there. She still has follow-up appointments. After that, I don't know." She went on, "I resigned my commission. There's nothing there now except the past. There's friends, of course, but their lives revolve around the air force." She stopped. "I don't know why I'm babbling about this." Her gaze met his. Electricity ran between them, sparking and sizzling in ways that baffled her. She swallowed hard, then tried to break the spell. "I'm not used to being aimless," she admitted.

"I understand that," he said, then asked, "Do you feel comfortable riding outside a ring? The instructor will be busy with Jenny for a while."

"I think it depends on the horse," she said cautiously.

He looked at his watch. "I can find one for you. It'll be an hour before Julie finishes the lesson and cools down Snowflake. There's two more parents arriving but they shouldn't be here before noon." He paused, then added, "Would you like to see more of the ranch on horseback?"

Don't go, a voice inside warned her.

Instead, she nodded and hoped she wouldn't make a fool out of herself in any of several ways.

"Why don't you watch Julie while I saddle the horses," he said.

She did at a distance, even though she was racked with doubts about going with him. What would Julie think if she saw them? But it was a simple ride, a short one that would be offered to any of the parents.

He returned quickly, leading two horses: a bay and a smaller roan. The bay, she knew, was Reese's horse. She knew from the size and the way the bay eagerly followed him. "This is Max," he said. "And this is Lady because she acts like one. She has very good manners."

Lauren hesitated, torn again. She wanted to watch her daughter ride but she knew she would see her again this afternoon when all four of the kids would perform. She decided she would only distract her daughter if Julie saw her now.

"Lady wasn't chosen?" she asked.

"She's a family horse," he explained. "My sister rides her in parades. Nothing startles her."

"Won't your sister object?"

"No. She has another horse for everyday riding. She'll be happy that Lady is exercised today."

Max remained still, reins resting on the saddle horn, as Reese offered to help her mount. She shook her head, took the reins and easily swung into the saddle.

"I'm impressed," he said as he adjusted the stirrups. Then he asked, "How does the saddle feel?"

"Good. Your friend in Covenant Falls is a good teacher."

"Have you ridden outside a ring?"

"Once," she said.

"Can you trot?"

"Barely."

"Okay. Let's try a fast walk, then a trot. We're heading toward the pasture beyond the mustang compound."

His voice was confident, which gave her confidence. She knew she didn't have to impress him. He was a teacher by instinct. Her nervousness faded as they walked past the smaller stables and paddock for the mustangs. Leo followed at Max's heels.

After they passed the stables, she noticed the paddock for the mustangs had been divided by movable fencing. She was too occupied with riding to ask about it. They followed a well-worn path through what looked like pastureland, then headed through a series of gates. He leaned over to unlatch them in graceful movements. "We have to move the cattle around," he said, "so we don't wear out the land. Most of the cattle are in a valley on land we lease from the government. We move them closer in during the winter months."

They continued to ride past a pasture dotted with cattle. A stream of water tumbled from one of the cliffs that sheltered it. It wasn't a waterfall like Covenant Falls, just enough of a trickle to keep the valley green. Cattle grazed contentedly as one cowhand on a horse watched over them. Reese waved at him, and the man nodded.

"It's beautiful," she said.

"Look up," he said. She did and saw an eagle soaring above, then another.

"They're so graceful."

"They are that, and they're also predators. We have to move moms with young calves to a safe paddock that's constantly watched."

His words conjured a picture she tried to erase, but it

was a part of his world. She changed the subject. "How long has your family owned the ranch?"

"A hundred and fifty years, give or take a few. We don't know exactly. The founder was Henry Howard, one of the legendary mountain men and apparently illiterate. Much of what we know comes from stories told by one generation to another. According to the legend, he was out of water and starving and followed an eagle into the valley, figuring that there must be water and game here.

"We assume," he continued, "mostly because we want to, that our eagles are descended from the original ones who led Henry into the valley."

"I like that story," she said. "Then what happened?"

"Patti didn't tell you?"

"No."

"Henry didn't like people much, from all reports. But as he grew older, he knew he needed help and bought a mail-order bride. Paid for her traveling expenses and married her the day she arrived in Denver. He arranged it through one of his few friends."

She was spellbound. Why hadn't Patti told her the story? It was something right out of a book, but then she'd always believed truth was often stranger than fiction. "Then what?"

"He brought her back here. I imagine she was rather horrified. It couldn't have been much more than a shack, but she was an orphan and ambitious and pushed her husband into buying a couple of cows. That's how it started."

"And they lived happily ever after?"

"They must have. According to her bible, there were five children. Two were killed by Utes during an uprising. Two apparently wandered off on their own adventures and were never heard of again. I take it the original Howard was not an easy man to live with. One was left to build the ranch."

"That's a great story," she said. "Patti said you were one-fourth Ute."

"True. I'm proud of it. Apparently, my grandmother was a very caring, beautiful woman. She was a doctor in a time when it was rare for a Ute woman. She died in an accident before I was born. They had one son, my father. My grandfather never remarried, which is why my family tree is pretty thin.

"Now it's your turn," he said. "How did you become a fighter pilot?"

"Long story," she said. "My mother was a single mom. I never knew my birth father. She never spoke of him. She was a great mother, though. Never went to college but worked two or three jobs to make sure I had food and clothes and love.

"One day, when I was ten or so," she continued, "I looked up and saw a plane streak across the sky just as a ray of sun turned it into gold. I knew then that I wanted to fly. I started reading books about flying. When I was sixteen I worked in an ice cream shop after school during weekdays and at the library on Saturdays. I didn't make as much there, but I loved books and particularly books about flying.

"Then one day an older man—his name was Hank Douglas—came to the counter and asked the librarian for novels about flying. She knew my interests and sent him to me. I recommended several and he came back the next Saturday and told me how everything in them was wrong and why. I recommended a few more, and we became friends.

"I told him I'd never been in a plane, but that some-day I wanted to be a pilot. He recognized the hunger in me and asked if I wanted to go up in his two-seater. I knew my mom would never approve, so I didn't tell her. I didn't think it was exactly a lie, more of an omission.

"I read mysteries, too, though, so I wrote a note as to where I was going and with whom and tucked it in a book next to my bed. I figured that if he wasn't the good guy I thought he was, I could tell him about the note—that there was a way for others to know my whereabouts."

Reese chuckled. "I'll have to remember that devious side of you."

"I didn't need it. He took me up in the air and I never wanted to come back down. He started teaching me to fly on afternoons I should have been working. He encouraged me to take more math and apply at the Air Force Academy. I had hoped for a scholarship, but I had never thought about the academy. To my amazement, I was accepted, and I think he had something to do with it.

"Life is full of small things—a glance at the sky, a chance meeting, a library book—that can change a life," she mused aloud.

"Did your mother ever know about the flying lessons?"

"No, I don't think so. She worked as a companion to an ill lady during the day and as a waitress in the evenings. She knew I spent a lot of time in the library when I wasn't in school or at the ice cream shop."

"Did she ever find out later on?"

"No. I didn't want her to know I'd lied to her. I might have told her eventually, but she died during my last year at the academy. That lie still weighs on my conscience…

And now I'm a mother, too, I worry myself sick about a fifteen-year-old daughter and what *I* don't know."

She bit her lip. "I never told anyone that before," she said as she suddenly realized there were tears in her eyes. She never cried. Even after the accident. Sometimes, things hurt too much to cry. *Why now? Why with him?*

He leaned over Max and wiped a tear away. "I'm sorry," he said softly. "I think she would be very proud of you."

Lauren wasn't so sure. Her mom was a bear on the question of honesty. "We should get back."

He nodded. "Want to try a canter?" he asked.

She tried a smile. "Maybe a slow one."

His right hand raised her chin until her eyes met his. "You have the most striking eyes, and I hate seeing tears in them. I'm sorry I asked."

"I never told that story about the lessons to anyone before," she said. "Not even…Dane."

"We all have those haunting pieces of our lives," he said and leaned down and kissed her. Lightly. As if for comfort. Not passion.

And, to her surprise, it *was* comforting. Something she'd lived with for years was released in that moment. She wondered what his haunting moment was.

She didn't have time to think. He turned his horse, and she followed. There was no more talk as they cantered back to the stables.

Her daughter and Jenny were still in the ring when they returned. He dismounted first, outside the stables, and waited for her. She swung her leg over but slipped as she dismounted. He caught her as she stumbled against the horse. For the barest second, she leaned against him. Electricity ran through her, then guilt. She jerked away.

She shouldn't feel this way. It was…disloyal. Wrong. She straightened and brushed a wisp of hair from her forehead. "I'm…sorry."

"No need. It happens often when you're not that used to riding. It's a big step down."

But she knew from his expression that he'd felt something, too. She tried to normalize her voice. "Shall I take care of the horse?"

"Nope. Parents are guests. We take care of guests."

She started to turn away.

"Luke's doing a great job," he said with a slow smile that could seduce a saint.

Confusion flooded her until she realized he meant her riding instructor in Covenant Falls and he was complimenting her on her riding. Then she felt so many things. Pride at the compliment. Shock that she had told him her deepest secret, and a warmth that was building inside her. "Thank you," she managed. But she couldn't move. Silence stretched tautly between them.

Just then a car approached, and a wry smile crossed Reese's lips. "That's Jenny's father," he said. "I'll introduce you after you see your daughter."

She turned around. Julie had disappeared into the stable from the ring. Lauren went inside and found her unsaddling Snowflake. To her surprise, Julie gave her a huge hug.

"Did you see me?" her daughter asked.

"I did, and I am so proud of you," Lauren said. She stepped back. "You looked really, really good, and I love the pink in those cheeks."

"That's sunburn," Julie said. "I saw you on a horse, too." It was more a question than a statement.

"I've been going to riding school, too. In Covenant

Falls," Lauren said. "I thought I would learn something about horses so we can ride together in the future. And I've been investigating places we can visit when you're through."

"You think, maybe, we can get a horse?" Julie said hopefully.

She would have given Julie the moon at that moment if she could. Since she couldn't, she would do her best to get the dog and try to arrange something to do with a horse. A house near some stables maybe. But right now she was delighted to see the wide grin on Julie's face she'd missed so much.

Chapter 9

Sunday morning passed much too quickly. The other parents started arriving at noon, and the teens put on a show.

They started slowly, riding their horses around the ring, first walking, followed by a fast walk, a trot and a canter.

Under an increasingly ominous-looking sky, they then executed perfect figure eights, turning their mounts in various exercises. Best of all, the four looked proud and happy. It might have been parental pride, but Lauren thought her Julie outshone the others. That, though, wasn't the purpose of the program.

The goal had been to build confidence in the riders, and she watched the results. There was an assurance about them that was impressive.

Her gaze kept moving toward Reese. He was everywhere, encouraging the kids as they went through their routines and then praising them when they finished.

She knew the next steps in the program from the information she'd received. They would continue to gain confidence, practice the different gaits and gain more control of their horses. They would leave the paddock for longer rides, both in groups, and with their buddy. And, more exciting to them, start working with the mustangs.

After the riding exhibition, Reese explained the next steps to the parents: the introduction of their teen to a mustang while continuing to build their horsemanship skills. "The mustangs will be in different pens. One teen will be assigned to each horse. They'll spend a minimum of four hours a day with their mustang. Your son or daughter can read, sing or talk to the mustangs.

"The first success will come when the horse approaches their new friend and accepts carrots from them. There will always be a trained ranch hand nearby.

"So far," he continued, "only myself and my foreman have interacted with the mustangs. We provided food and water but they still run from us. But for some reason no one really understands, the mustangs relate to younger humans."

Lauren knew there was more to it than that. From all her reading on the subject, she learned wild horses seemed to respond especially well to humans with emotional or physical wounds. They sense a need that calms their fears.

Reese continued, "When the teen's mustang loses the fear of him or her, it makes it easier for one of the experienced horsemen to start training the horse, first with the halter, followed by a blanket, then harness and saddle, then to walk on a lead and finally tolerate a rider. Your teen will be learning training techniques as well as riding ability."

The families scattered then as each teen took his or her family to the stable to meet their horse.

After giving the families time to visit, it was nearly three when Reese announced the cookout was ready, after which there would be a brief ceremony awarding each of the students a silver horseshoe pin for succeeding in the first phase of basic horsemanship.

A buffet meal was set out on tables in front of the main house. As Lauren approached, she found a large pot of chili, a large salad heavily loaded with different greens, tomatoes, olives and other veggies, homemade fresh, hot bread and a giant platter of sliced roast beef. Apple pie rounded out the meal.

Lauren noted with amazement that her daughter took a big bowl of chili and turned back to her. "This is the best chili ever," Julie said, as she dumped a pile of salad and roast beef onto her plate.

Lauren couldn't remember when her daughter had selected so much, not even when she was running and needed calories, and especially not since the accident. Lauren heaped her plate as well and discovered why Julie's appetite had improved.

Her daughter was already brimming over with horse lore as she ate. She'd always been a good student and now she was bursting with newly discovered information. "Did you know that you can tell whether a horse is in a relaxed, playful mood rather than an impulsive, survive-at-any-cost mood?" she asked her mother.

"I did not," Lauren admitted.

"When he's relaxed, his neck and head are level," she said. "The eyes are soft and curious. When he's scared, adrenaline rushes through him. His body is tense and braced, his head and neck are elevated, his nostrils are flared and his eyes are open wide. Our job," she added proudly, "is to relax our horse so the trainer can work."

Lauren hadn't seen her daughter so animated since she'd won a major track race. Her eyes fairly sparkled. The change in her was startling. She saw similar conversations were transpiring between the other families.

She talked to several of the other families as they finished the meal. They had a lot in common. All were military families who had lost a husband or wife, mom or dad.

Tony's mother was the most talkative. As soon as her son left the table to talk with another boy, she boasted about her son's newly acquired skills. "I'm so glad he's found something he likes," the woman said. "He's not one for schoolwork, but he's real excited about working with horses."

Reese joined the group then with a young man at his side. "This is Nathan," he said. "My nephew. He was herding cattle last Sunday but he's here to stay and help throughout the program now."

Nathan nodded to her. "You have an equestrian here, Mrs. MacInnes," he said to Lauren, "and that's despite the fact she can't really use her left leg with the horse. They seem to understand each other."

Julie beamed as he smiled at her. He was a good-looking boy who had the same dark eyes and rangy build as his uncle.

Lauren tried to push a sudden concern aside and move the conversation to new territory. "The food was delicious but there was a lot of it," she said.

"Between the guests, the kids and the staff, it'll be gone before you can blink," Reese said. "There's more that has gone to the bunkhouse."

"How do the boys like the bunkhouse?" Lauren asked.

"They love it. Not too many kids can say they stayed in a real Western bunkhouse and trained mustangs."

"It doesn't bother your cowhands?"

He shook his head. "Gives them a chance to show off," he said, "and be big brothers for a month."

Just as he said the words, thunder roared through the valley and a few raindrops started falling.

"Let's get everything inside," Sally said. "Storms up here come fast and strong." Without being asked, the teens and parents immediately started taking in food and stacking the chairs and taking them to the barn.

Tony's and Jenny's parents had driven up together from Denver and decided to leave immediately.

Heath's uncle asked if he could stay overnight in the bunkhouse since he had a longer drive by himself. Reese readily agreed and turned to Lauren. "I think you should stay, too. That road can be slippery and difficult in a storm. We have several spare bedrooms."

She hesitated. She didn't have any clothes with her other than what she was wearing. But when she looked back at the angry sky, she knew she didn't want to go down that winding road in a driving rain, particularly when it was dark.

That meant, though, spending more time with her daughter, and Reese. Not wise, but she didn't have much of a choice. "Thanks," she said. "I'll take you up on that, but I don't have anything else with me."

"I think we can fill in a few items," Reese said. "We've been known to have guests snowed in, and we keep emergency packages for them. Just simple things like toothbrushes, toothpaste, shampoo. Sally has extra jackets you can use. It could get colder tonight. If you want to help, you can keep the kids occupied. All my

people will be busy, and it can get scary in the house
when the thunder roars."

She wasn't sure at all whether that was a good idea.
Her only experience with kids was her daughter and she
hadn't been great at that. But she nodded her head. "I
can do that. What about you?"

"I'm going to help my crew get the horses inside their
stalls. Several of my guys will probably have to go out
tonight to calm the cattle if the weather takes a turn for
the worse," Reese said as he pulled on a long yellow
raincoat with a split in back.

"I should call the inn. The way news spreads in town,
someone might worry if I simply disappear in a rain-
storm. Apparently, everyone looks after everyone else,
and since the poker game, I'm one of them."

"I doubt there's any cell service now. You can use the
office computer to send an email. Hopefully, it will be
working. We've been having some problems with it."

"About the kids," she reminded him, "the only game
I know is poker."

"So teach them," he said. "It's something every kid
needs to know for future reference."

"Can I keep the proceeds?"

He chuckled. "Depends on what you play for."

"I have complete freedom?"

"I'll trust your good judgment."

"Do you have chips and cards?"

"That's like asking a pro football player if he has a
football."

"You're that good?"

"Remember I've played in Covenant Falls, too."

"What about Heath's uncle?" she asked.

"Sally will look after him."

"And your nephew?"

"He'll be working with us. Which reminds me I have to go."

"Be careful!"

He nodded. It was obvious he was worried.

She went inside and watched from the window as ranch hands brought horses in from several paddocks situated around the ranch as the thunder grew louder and took them into two different stables. The mustangs had already been driven inside their stable earlier in the day because of the visitors.

Lauren went into the kitchen where Sally and Betty were putting food away and making a huge urn of coffee. "These sudden summer storms can be bad," Sally said.

"Why put all the horses in the stables?"

"We always do when there's thunder. Some are easily frightened by storms, particularly if there's lightning. You get one running, and the others might follow and crash through fences."

She nodded.

"Betty can finish up. Let me show you your room."

Lauren followed Sally up a flight of stairs.

"Julie and Jenny—the boys are calling them the Two Js—are to the left," Sally said. "They have adjoining rooms connected by a bathroom. You'll be to the right. A bathroom is next door and you'll be the only one using it."

Sally opened a door and stood aside as Lauren went inside. The room was like much of the ranch. Simple. Homey. The large bed was covered with a thick comforter. A window overlooked the stables. The bathroom next door had both a bathtub with a shower fixture and plenty of fluffy towels.

It looked inviting. She only wished she had come prepared for an overnight stay, but how did you predict a sudden mountain storm? She did have her purse. After Sally left, Lauren washed her face and hands and wished she had something else to wear.

She went back downstairs. The living room was spacious and furnished for comfort rather than fashion. Big cushy chairs and a plush sofa large enough to comfortably seat six people occupied the center of the room. A huge fireplace took up one corner and a bookcase in another. Two game tables with chairs were placed next to large windows that looked out over the barn and meadow in back of the house.

She went to one of the windows. Although it was only a little after five, the room was darkening. Great bulbous clouds churned above, and rain was coming down hard now. She saw figures outside taking horses into the barn. In the distance she saw a streak of lightning.

"Reese said you wanted to contact the inn," Sally said. She led Lauren out of the living room and two more doors down. "This is the office. The landline is working, so you might try that. The computer can be a little stubborn sometimes."

Lauren looked around. It was a medium-size room. Lauren noted file cabinets covering one side and a bookcase filled with stimulating titles such as *Ranch Management*, *Today's Ranching* and *A Hard Look at Today's Cowboy*. There were also neatly stacked piles of folders on a table next to the computer.

"Thanks," she said.

"When you get through, why don't you join me in the kitchen for a cup of coffee."

"Reese asked if I could help out with the teens."

"That would be terrific. All the ranch hands are busy,

and I'll be, as well. Oh, and will you need any clothes tonight?"

She could live with what she had for a day or two. She'd certainly done it as a cadet and pilot.

"I'm fine with a new toothbrush," she said. "But I do need a deck of cards or two if you have them."

"Cards are in a compartment of the game table," Sally replied. "As far as clothes go, I'll put a duster in your room. We can wash your clothes tomorrow. How does that sound?"

"Good."

After Sally left, Lauren tried the landline and reached the inn. She reported her situation. Then she tried the computer, and it worked. She found her purse, took out several bills along with a quarter, a nickel and a dime. She photographed each with her cell phone, and emailed the images to herself, then played with them on the computer. She made the coins larger. She added color, the coins being bronze and the bills being green. Then she printed copies of them. She cut out the dollar bills and then carefully cut the quarters into squares and the dimes and nickels into smaller squares to represent those coins.

They were paper, of course, but at least they represented the originals.

Sally returned with a cup of coffee. "Since you were busy, I thought I would bring coffee to you." She glanced at the computer-produced money. "You did that? On the computer?"

"Sure. You want to join us? There's more than enough money, and I can always make more."

Sally grinned. "I'm tempted but I think it should just be the four. It should have been their night and I suspect you'll make a great dealer. I also have a lot of cold, wet people needing coffee and food."

"You think it's okay to play poker?" Lauren asked. She'd worried that it might be inappropriate. It was, though, one of the few games she knew.

Sally shrugged. "It's a game. You don't keep people from watching football because people gamble on it. It might not hurt if you threw in a few precautionary notes."

Lauren nodded. Sally left, and Lauren picked up the money and walked into the game room. The teens apparently had been told to meet there, and they looked up at her expectantly, all except her daughter, who looked as if she wanted to hide under the nearest cushion.

It was Tony who spoke first. "I heard you were a fighter pilot. Are there many women fighter pilots?"

"There's a growing number of us," she said.

"Why did you decide to be one?" Jenny asked softly.

"I liked to fly," she said. "A very nice pilot took me up in a small plane one day when I was a bit younger than you, and I decided I belonged there. The best way to do that was through the Air Force Academy."

"My mom was a helicopter pilot," Jenny offered.

"You should be very proud of her," Lauren said. "The chopper pilots have the most dangerous jobs and are incredibly brave," she added. "They come and rescue us when we go down, no matter how dangerous it is. No one has more respect for chopper pilots than fixed wing pilots." She looked around the table. "You all should be proud of your parents." She brought them to a different topic. "Okay, who has the best horse here?"

As she expected they all raised their hands. "Okay, I know about Snowflake. Tony, who did you pick and why?"

"Andy," he said. "He made little eager snorting noises, and he nuzzled me even before I picked him. It was kinda like 'I want *you*.'"

She turned to Heath. "Heath?"

"My horse is Checkers," he said. "I picked him because he was a black-and-white mustang. He's a really good horse now. He was one of the wild mustangs the last kids worked with."

"Jenny?"

"I picked Cindy for Cinderella. She looked...shy."

"And quite pretty," Lauren said. "I watched you today. You were really good. All of you were."

Her daughter raised her eyebrows with that "do you have to do that?" look.

Lauren ignored it. "Well, from what I saw today, you all picked winners. You looked great, a lot better than I looked a few days ago when I took a riding lesson."

They were beginning to relax. She made her next pitch. "I know this was supposed to be a celebration tonight for all your hard work, but I guess the sky is celebrating for you with its fireworks," she said.

"With a wet blanket," quipped Heath.

"Ah, we have a comic," Lauren said. She tipped her head. "That was really pretty clever."

Heath beamed.

"Since the celebration is temporarily postponed," she said, "does anyone have an idea of what game you want to play? Scrabble, maybe?"

As she expected, no one looked excited other than her daughter. She suspected Julie had already outplayed them all. "Or," she added, "we can play hearts."

"That's lame," Heath contributed. "What about something interesting like poker?"

He meant it as a joke. She'd hoped someone would pop up with it so she wouldn't have to.

"That's a possibility," she said slowly. "I just happen to have some money with me."

"I like hearts," Jenny said.

"Poker," Julie said. "My dad taught me."

Lauren was stunned. It was said easily. Without tears. And with pride. It was the first time Julie had mentioned Dane without tearing up.

"Tony?" Lauren asked.

Tony glanced at Jenny, and Lauren wondered whether a teen relationship was forming. "I guess I have to say poker," he finally said.

"That okay with you, Jenny?"

"I don't know how to play."

"I'll help you, then," Lauren said. "And since I would probably get arrested if you played with real money, I manufactured some on the computer down the hall. Just in case you wanted to play." She passed out ten dollars in paper money to each of the teens.

"Whoever is the big winner," she said, "has bragging rights."

"That's all?" Heath asked.

"And learn or improve a skill," she added. "It comes in handy. The idea, though, is it's a social game. I played Monday night in an all-veteran Covenant Falls poker game. I didn't know anyone when I went in. I had fifteen friends when I came out. I modestly say I won. Guess how much?"

They went through numbers, ranging from fifty to a hundred.

"About seven dollars, but the real thing I won was three hours of pleasure and new friendships. Okay?"

As rain beat against the windows, and lightning darted across the sky, the four teenagers became absorbed in the game. Lauren played the role of dealer and helped Jenny. Sally brought in some munchies and lemonade, which seemed to be her go-to drink. The game broke up at ten when Reese came in, Leo by his side. The latter went around the table, greeting each one and shaking water all over them. No one seemed to mind.

Reese was soaked when he came into the room. Water dripped from his mussed hair. He'd taken off his boots but his socks were wet as were the legs of his jeans.

Reese looked at the fake money lying on the game table. "What is this?"

"We're playing poker," Heath said. "Mrs. MacInnes made the money on the computer."

"You did this? How?" he asked her as he picked up one of the dollars.

"I used my cell phone to take photos of money in my wallet," she said, "and played around with them on the computer. I hope that was okay. Sally thought it was a good idea."

He furrowed his brows, uttered something that might have had a "damn" in it.

"I hope that wasn't wrong," she said anxiously.

"No," he said. "I'm just surprised. Who's winning?"

"I am," Jenny said quietly. The boys looked abashed but, to Lauren's delight, her daughter just nodded her head and smiled.

Lauren felt a satisfaction she'd not felt in a long time. *The teens are turning into a team.*

Reese stood there, dripping. "I have bad news," he said.

They all looked at him.

"We'll have to cancel meeting the mustangs tomorrow."
Faces fell.

"The rain is beginning to flood one of our pastures.
We have to take cattle to a higher one tonight. It'll take
most of the ranch hands and we'll be out all night and
most of tomorrow. They're getting ready now."

He paused, then looked at the boys and added, "You
can sleep in the house tonight. You can get your stuff,
and Sally will show you the room. The bunkhouse will
be pretty busy. Heath, your dad will stay here, as well.
He's helping out in the kitchen.

"I'm not sure how we'll handle tomorrow," he continued. "I doubt the instructors will get here. I'm hoping
Sally and Burt Ames, one of our best riders, can work
with you in the riding barn in back of the house. It ap-
pears the rain will last most of tomorrow."

The teens looked disappointed but nodded.

It was obviously a message to leave. The teens said
good-night and filed out. Julie waited until the others
left and grinned at her. "Good job, Mom," she said as
she left the room.

Reese lingered as they left. "Well, that poker game
was obviously a big hit," he said, sitting next to her. "It
was better than anything I would propose. I would have
gone with some kid's game…and they would have been
bored to death and worried about the horses."

She felt better about her choice. "It's going to be a
rough night for you, isn't it?"

He nodded. "I'm afraid so," he said. "It's going to be
a hard rain all night. That damn thunder's the big problem, though, particularly with the cattle. They're apt to
run and crash through fences and then there's the flood-

ing. I'm just sorry for the kids. I know how much they've been anticipating meeting their mustangs."

"I could see the disappointment on their faces when you told them, but you *did* want them to experience ranch life," Lauren said. "They should know this is part of it."

He hesitated. "I hate to ask, but can you stay over tomorrow and look after them? Sally and Betty will be busy getting food to us, and you seem to have a way with the kids."

She raised an eyebrow. "Not that I know of," she said. "Julie was always her father's daughter. She and I have never…communicated like she did with Dane."

"That's not what I've seen," he said. "She talks about you frequently. She's very proud of you."

That can't be right. "That's good to hear, but…"

He put a finger on her lips, then put his arms around her, his fingers kneading the back of her neck. She found herself leaning into him. She looked up into his face, unable to take her gaze away.

"You have no idea how delectable you looked when you were concentrating on that poker game with the kids."

She furrowed her brow in puzzlement. "Why?"

"You give everything in you to whatever you're doing at the time. Even a poker game with kids. You went to the trouble of creating the money, and damn, I'm still not sure how you did it."

Her heart beat faster. He'd seemed the essence of strength and confidence, and yet in the past few minutes he'd seemed somehow vulnerable. He bent his head, and his lips met hers. Every nerve in her started to tingle. The kiss deepened, taking on a wild, fierce quality that made everything else fade into nothingness.

She closed her eyes, letting herself know sensuality again for the first time in more than sixteen months. It felt right. But was it right? How could she feel so strongly about a man she barely knew? She swallowed hard and eased back.

His dark eyes searched hers. "Too soon?" he asked as he dropped his hands from her back and pushed back a curl that had fallen on her forehead.

She didn't reply. His warmth felt too good, the concern in his eyes too caring. Instead, she leaned into him to feel the hard planes of his body, the strength that was there. She stayed there as his arms went around her again.

"I don't know," she said bluntly. "I'm attracted to you. Obviously. But I feel like I'm jumping off a cliff without knowing how deep the chasm is."

"It can be very deep," he replied slowly as he played with a ringlet of her hair. "I love this ranch and I love the mountains. I love the winters, but they can be long, cold and lonely for someone who is accustomed to living in a city."

It was then she saw grief engraved in his face.

It disappeared so quickly she thought she might have imagined it. He stood and gave her a hand up. "I like you, Mrs. MacInnes. I like you very much. Too much, I'm afraid. It confuses me," he added with a crooked smile.

"Me, too," she said. "When the storm clears, I should leave…"

"Don't make any decisions now," he said. He reached down and kissed her forehead. Gently. Comfortingly. "I should get back. We have a long night ahead."

She was wordless as he moved away. She didn't want him to go. She wanted him to stay and persuade her.

Hells bells, she didn't know what she wanted. Her feelings were all mixed up.

So much for the cool, confident pilot she had been.

"Thanks for what you did with the kids tonight," he said gently. "They will be telling their friends for years that they played poker with a fighter pilot."

She smiled. "You're going now?"

"We'll grab something to eat," he said. "Both Chet and I will be out all night. If there's as much thunder and lightning as I'm afraid there might be, it's going to be rough. Cows don't like thunder, and the flooding looks bad."

He touched her chin and their gazes met. She felt hypnotized by his dark eyes. "We really do need you for the next several days."

"I…I'll do what I can. But you…"

"You'll stay?"

"As long as I'm needed," she said. "Stay safe."

She caught herself then. It was always what she and Dane told each other when scheduled for a flight.

"I will." He gave her a crooked smile, then walked out. The room suddenly felt cold.

She walked over and peered out a window. She watched for several minutes before she saw him leave the house and mount a horse Chet was holding for him. He was in the long rain duster with the brim of his hat pulled down to protect his eyes from the rain that was driving down steadily.

She kept watching while he and seven other men disappeared into the rain.

Chapter 10

Lauren tore herself away from the window and went into the kitchen.

It was bustling.

Betty was baking something that smelled wonderful and a woman she didn't know was busy filling thermoses with coffee and soup.

"Care packages for the drovers," Sally explained. "The black thermoses are filled with coffee, the red ones with chicken soup. Darn almanac was wrong. It said no rain today." She turned to the woman next to her. "Meet Ann, Chet's wife. Ann, meet Lauren."

"Hi," Ann said. "I'm glad to meet you, although not this way. Chet's talked a lot about you."

"Ann!" Sally cut her off quickly. "Are you through with that bunch of sandwiches?"

"I am," Ann said. "And I'm going into the dining

room to sit down." She grinned at Lauren. "I'm pregnant."

"That's wonderful," Lauren said. "Congratulations."

When she left, Sally lowered her voice. "She's going to stay in one of the rooms upstairs tonight. We don't want her alone tonight during the storm."

"How bad is it?"

"Real bad. The winter feeding pasture they'll move the cattle to isn't close, and they have to go through some rough areas, and calves have a habit of wandering off. Keeping them together is the hard part. The thunder and lightning don't help."

"Chet and Reese seem close." It was more a statement than a question.

"They are. Chet was born here. Chet's father worked for our father. The boys grew up together. They're closer than a lot of brothers I know. Chet and Ann have a house on a creek about half a mile from here."

"And Chet's father?"

She shrugged.

Lauren guessed that wasn't a happy subject. "Reese asked me to look after the kids tomorrow."

"They're fine for tonight, thanks to you," Sally said. "It's tomorrow that's the problem. They were really looking forward to the mustangs tomorrow, but that's out of the question now. So is any riding. Every one of our hands is doing double duty now and we can't spare any of them to teach or be there for safety reasons."

"I'll come up with something," Lauren said. She just didn't know what. She'd used the poker card. She didn't think another day of poker would be much of a worthy pastime. Neither did she think the boys would enjoy a day of Scrabble or playing other card games when ranch hands were outside in driving rain trying to save cattle.

Lauren finally got up and went upstairs. It had been a far longer day than she'd anticipated when she left Covenant Falls early this morning.

She took a long, hot shower, then dropped into bed, but the rain pounding against the windows and the intermittent lightning kept her mind on the men slogging through the weather, particularly one in a yellow duster.

Sleep didn't come easily. Reese's kiss was still engraved in her thoughts, and the faces of two men kept popping in and out. How could she have feelings for one when those for the other were still alive?

She woke up as gray light entered the room. She looked at the clock. It was 6:00 a.m.

She stood up, wishing she had a robe. Instead, she wrapped a large towel she'd taken from the bathroom last night and wrapped it around her and walked over to the window. The rain was still coming down hard. It was oddly quiet beneath the window.

She opened the door and found a bundle of clothes. There was the promised duster, which would do in the room, a pair of jeans that looked as if they'd never been worn and a red-and-white-checkered shirt. There was also a belt for the jeans.

It was needed. The shirt was large but fine. The jeans were held up only because of the belt.

It was 6:30 a.m. by the time she got downstairs, and the kitchen was buzzing with activity. Sally was packing sandwiches, Betty was baking something that smelled wonderful and Ann was busy filling more thermoses with coffee.

"Reese and Chet are still out?" Lauren asked.

"Afraid so. They've been out there all night and will be gone most of the day. It takes time, but they should be back sometime tonight. We're sending supplies via pack horse." She looked at the ill-fitting jeans. "I was afraid of that. You can use our washer and dryer for your own clothes. It's at the back of this room."

"Thanks, I'll do that but in the meantime I appreciate the loan," Lauren said. "What about the mustangs?" Lauren asked.

"They're in their stables," Sally said. "Reese and Chet are the only ones who can handle them safely, so the horses will stay there. They'll be fed and watered by Nathan. It's safe enough when they're in the stalls."

"Maybe the teens can pitch in by cleaning the stable, not just for their horses but for all those who are out in this weather," Lauren suggested. "Your ranch hands probably didn't have time to clean their stalls out before leaving. We can put feed and water in them. When they return, we can meet them and take care of their horses."

"That's a terrific idea," Sally said. "They're going to be exhausted when they arrive. But will the kids go for it? There are twenty stalls. It's asking a lot."

"We should make it an adventure," Lauren said. "And maybe even have a prize. Like who can clean a stall the fastest? And," she added, "Reese said he wanted them to experience ranch life. This is part of it."

"What would the prizes be?" Betty asked.

"The winner could pick the meal for a day, or a dessert, or a game or an outing. They would be helping the ranch hands at the same time. I think this group is competitive. They certainly were at their poker game."

"Wouldn't your daughter be at a disadvantage?" Sally asked. "She doesn't have the same mobility as the others do."

"Don't tell her that. She's the most competitive person I know. It faded for a while but you all are bringing it back. And her mobility is getting better day by day," Lauren added. "I don't want her to think of what she can't do, but what she *can* do."

"It's worth a try," Sally said. "They would be pitching in where there's a need. A good lesson. I know the hands would appreciate it. They're going to be dead tired when they come in. They get no sleep on one of these drives."

"What about asking the kids when they come down?" Lauren said, words tumbling out as she thought out loud. "Somehow make it their idea. Present it as a gift to the ranch hands who have helped them so much."

"Winner gets to pick a meal within limits," Betty said. "No pizza three times that day. Once, maybe… But I like it. You have a devious mind, Mrs. MacInnes. I admire that. It'll keep them busy on a rainy day."

"Call me Lauren," she said. "I should return to Covenant Falls," she said. "All my clothes and other belongings are there."

"The roads are going to be bad for the next day or so. Several of them will probably be flooded," Sally said. "You can call the inn when we have service again and ask them to pack your clothes and hold them until you return. They're very accommodating."

Lauren thought about it. She realized she didn't want to leave. For the first time since the accident, she felt closer to her daughter. She liked being around horses and people who liked them. She liked Leo. She liked

Sally and Betty and Chet. She wanted to watch as they trained the mustangs.

She tried to ignore the fact that she would also see more of Reese.

Reese was cold, tired and frustrated.

The cattle did not go willingly. There was good grass and water where they were. They did not understand that the water was rising as overfed streams started spilling over their banks. And then there was always that pesky calf that wandered off. Leo was a good cattle dog and could usually bring them back, but it slowed the drive.

A horse-drawn wagon following the drovers carried portable fencing to keep the cattle from wandering once they reached their new temporary home. Reese didn't like using that pasture. It was too far from the ranch house and several of his hands had to stay with them. None of them liked it. It was a lonely business. The destination was land leased from the federal government. Not really theirs.

He had time to think on the ride up, particularly about Lauren. Too much time. He'd wanted to kiss her earlier. He would swear she felt the same way. There had been a strong attraction between them since they'd met. After the first ten minutes of their initial meeting, he'd liked her, and that like had grown exponentially. There was a subtle humor hidden in a very self-contained exterior. And strength.

He liked the way she handled the kids as adults. He liked the way she cared about her daughter enough to give up a profession she loved. He'd been fascinated to find her teaching poker and how much the teens had enjoyed being treated like grown-ups.

He'd not been seriously interested in a woman since Cara and the pain and disaster that resulted from their marriage. He'd been smitten from the moment he met Cara Taylor. She, too, was smart and attractive. They fell in love quickly. Too quickly, as it turned out. Both of them paid a high price for the speed.

He vowed then never to make the same mistake. And sure, he'd been tempted. He wanted children, but he wanted a good, solid home for them with friends and opportunities. He had to admit there wasn't much of either at Eagles' Roost...

Reese, his crew and Leo returned to the house and stables at around nine Monday night. It had stopped raining but the trees were still dripping. The ranch hands were sopping wet, cold, hungry and tired. Reese was the first to approach the stable when Tony Fields met him. "I'll take care of your horse, sir," he said. "There's food and water in his stall."

Startled, Reese dismounted and watched with amazement as quiet Jenny took the next horse from a rider who gratefully surrendered the reins and started toward the bunkhouse. Heath took the third horse.

Julie stepped up then. "Mom and I will hold the other horses until the first ones are bedded down. All the stalls have been cleaned, and water and feed replenished. We'll finish unsaddling and warming your horses."

Reese wanted to protest but then he saw Lauren. She shook her head.

He nodded gratefully and signaled to the riders to dismount and go to the kitchen. "There's drinks and coffee, and food. Beer, too, for those who want it."

Nathan, who had been with them all day, hesitated. "I'll stay," he said. "They might need help."

"You're as wet as the rest of us," Reese pointed out.

"Yeah, but I'm younger," Nathan replied with a grin.

Reese hesitated, then with a slight smile said, "So you are. You don't have to rub it in. Go help them." He turned toward the kitchen. When he walked inside, he dropped his boots in the mudroom and soaked up the warmth. Once in the kitchen, he stripped off his gloves and took the coffee offered to him. The available beer was attractive but he needed the warmth of the coffee. A pot of stew was on the stove and a mound of several different types of sandwiches sat on a huge platter.

"What just happened?" he asked Sally. "Why are the kids in the stable?"

"They came to me this afternoon. I explained what was involved in moving cattle," Sally replied, "that it was a cold, wet, punishing drive. They wanted to do something to help and came up with the idea all by themselves. They've been out there cleaning stalls, refreshing water buckets and preparing the feed for each horse, according to the whiteboard. They cleaned the stalls and put down shavings. Even Heath's uncle pitched in for a few hours."

"How long have they been at it?"

"About five hours."

"*They* did all of that?" Chet asked suspiciously. "Who came up with the idea?"

"They didn't want to say. Apparently, it was group thought."

"Was Lauren, by any chance, with them?" Reese asked.

Sally looked up at the ceiling.

"Sally?"

"I think she might have been, but it was the kids who pushed the idea."

"I bet," Reese grumbled under his breath.

"Well, she might have mentioned they could help a little, but the kids enthusiastically came up with the idea of cleaning the stalls," she said, stumbling through her explanation. "You all taught them well," she added.

"Sally, you've been corrupted."

Chet interceded. "Well, they sure hit the target. I can't imagine anything more appreciated. We're dog-tired, wet and cold."

"That's what they figured," Sally said. "Get all the cattle out?"

"Pretty much," Reese said thoughtfully. "There's a few cows wandering about lost, but we'll take a couple of the guys tomorrow and gather the strays."

After nearly twenty hours in the saddle, the ranch hands usually dispersed quickly, but tonight they loitered while eating stew and munching sandwiches.

Lauren had stayed back when the riders reached the stable. She wanted to be there to help but she wanted the kids to take the lead. It had been Tony who came up with the plan after Sally explained what was happening. The others quickly agreed.

When they finished with the last horse, they trooped back into the house. With eight of them, including Nathan and Lauren, along with two ranch hands who had been left behind, it hadn't taken long to unsaddle the horses, rub them down and put warm blankets on them.

They all smelled like horse when they entered the kitchen and were met by a rousing cheer.

Reese held up a cup of steaming coffee in a salute, followed by those of his crew.

"Taking care of the horses meant a lot to us," Reese said. "Believe me when I say that, the proof being these people stayed here to say thank you rather than rushing to a shower and bed."

The words were followed by another round of "yahoos" from the men and two women behind him.

The teens, including her daughter, looked stunned, then stood a little straighter. Lauren suspected they weren't used to a lot of praise by adults. She vowed to herself she would do better.

Reese turned to business. "We'll have our ceremony for passing the first week with flying colors Wednesday night when everyone is awake. It might be a little later than planned and your parents won't be there, but you deserve it. As to getting back on schedule, Julie and Jenny will have their riding lessons in the morning, and the boys will work with their mustangs. You'll switch in the afternoon. And again, thank you for the homecoming surprise. I assure you it is greatly appreciated."

Another shout of approval came from the ranch hands, and then they started to disperse for the bunkhouse and showers, grabbing additional sandwiches as they did. After the last one, including Reese, left, the teens followed. Julie gave Lauren a big smile before following Jenny up to bed.

Lauren thought about lingering to see if Reese returned but realized he was dead tired and probably wanted nothing more than some sleep. She wasn't tired, though. She was exhilarated. She'd loved seeing the grateful faces on the incoming riders and the proud ones of the teens. She wasn't ready to go to bed.

She went into the corner library in the living room. Most of the books were old Westerns. She selected a classic and curled up in a big cushy chair. She was on the second chapter when Reese stepped inside. She knew it before she looked up and saw him. It was the musky male scent mixed with a tangy aftershave lotion.

He looked entirely different than he had a half hour earlier. He'd obviously taken a shower. His eyes were red, and lines of exhaustion were etched on his face as he sank into a chair near her.

"I thought you would be in bed," she said.

"I will be, before long."

"Rough night and day and night?"

"One of the lesser joys of ranching."

"And what are the big ones?"

"Watching a mare give birth. It's always a miracle to me." He took her hand in his. "And," he added, "nights like this. I was really proud of the kids tonight. Whose idea was it?"

"Does it matter?"

"No. What matters is they did it together and took pride in it. And the ranch hands appreciated it, probably more than you think. *I* appreciated it more than you'll know."

"You should probably go to bed," she suggested.

"I should," he agreed, "but I would rather talk to you. What are you reading?"

"A Western. I found it in the bookcase. *The Big Sky.*"

"It's a good one."

There was a pause as if he was considering whether he should say something more or not.

She tipped her head in question.

"I was impressed with what you did with the computer," he said.

The switch in topic made her head spin. She shrugged, "It was just play money and it wasn't that hard. And you certainly couldn't spend it. It's toy money."

He hesitated, then asked, "Are you good at math and contracts?"

Puzzled, she stared at him. "I'm good at math, have to be at the academy. Now contracts, not so much."

"But you are good on computers?"

"Aircraft are highly computerized these days," she said. "We have to know technology. Why?"

"Would you consider staying here longer?"

"Why?" she asked, puzzled, even if an odd expectation started poking her.

"I think I told you computers and I do not have a good relationship," Reese said.

"You did."

"Whenever I use one, something weird seems to happen. So I try not to use them. Sally isn't much better. Nathan has some skill but if something goes wrong, he's not much help, either."

"And?" she asked.

"You seem to understand the things," he said with that slow smile that charmed her. "Our bookkeeper, business manager and computer wizard is in Chicago because her mother is gravely ill. She was supposed to be back this week, but she called Sally earlier and her mother is worse. I don't know when she'll return, and we have some important bids and contracts going back and forth. We can't afford delays or mistakes. It wouldn't take much of your time."

She was stunned. "I don't know," she said. "As far as bookkeeping goes, I'm not so sure I'm your person."

"Anyone new would have a learning curve," he pressed. "Sandra could help you out via computer or phone. It would only be temporary."

Excitement filled her. She really liked the ranch. She liked the people who worked here. She loved the mountains. And it would be an intellectual challenge, one she badly needed.

And then there was Reese.

"I would have to ask Julie," she said. "I don't want to ruin this program for her. None of the other kids would have a parent hanging around."

"I wouldn't want that, either. Would you be comfortable talking to her about it?"

She wasn't sure, but excitement started to build in Lauren. She *was* good with computers. She had to be, since so many weapon systems were computerized. She'd felt aimless since she resigned her commission. She'd always needed goals and challenges.

The last week in Covenant Falls had been bearable because she'd been busy. She'd taken the riding lessons and did some exploring of the area but it wasn't what she wanted to do for weeks. She wanted to be involved in something worthwhile. Eagles' Roost's equine therapy program met that standard. So did the historic ranch.

And it would only be temporary.

He was regarding her steadily. "It might," he tempted, "bring you and your daughter closer. Riding is something you can have in common, and the other teens seem to really like you, not to mention all my employees after tonight."

"That was the kids tonight," she protested.

He raised an eyebrow. "I just wonder which one came up with the idea."

"It was a joint project," she said.

"I noticed you jumped in readily enough."

"Tony organized the work force."

He looked up, astonished. "Tony?"

"Yep, but don't let them know I spilled the beans. They wouldn't trust me again."

"I swear it," he said, "but I'm glad you told me. And you didn't answer my question. Will you consider staying here while Sandra's gone?"

It was a terrible idea. She knew it all the way through her bones. She couldn't stay away from Reese now.

"Don't you need some sleep?" she asked. Avoiding the answer.

"Yes, ma'am." He grinned at her. "You look swallowed up by those jeans."

"Which is why I'm driving to Covenant Falls in the morning," she shot back.

"But you look adorable."

They both stood. She was tall but he was a good six inches taller. She lifted her gaze to him, and his dark eyes seemed to smolder. He touched her cheek and ran his fingers along her cheekbone.

She turned her head slightly, and their lips met. Softly at first. Then hungrily as if they couldn't get enough of each other.

An internal voice warned her to stop.

But it was too late. As need and desire exploded between them she wondered whether from the moment they met if it had always been too late.

When his lips touched hers, she responded with all the need that had been building from the moment they first met. His kiss was not tentative but hungry. His arms locked around her as his mouth invited a response, even as his hands kneaded her back, sending ripples of sensation through her.

The quickening in her heart became a tattoo. It pounded so hard she knew he must hear it. There was something so solid about him, along with being immensely sexy. Her heart pounded an erratic rhythm as his kiss deepened, shaking her down to her toes. Torrents of sensation ran through her.

His arms tightened around her and she felt the quickened beat of his heart. He was compelling, had been since the first time they met. Maybe it was the toughness mixed with gentleness that so disarmed her. Maybe it was the time and heart he put into his mustang program or the way he worked with his employees. They not only respected him but also went way beyond what was expected of them. Maybe it was the dark eyes that hid emotions she was discovering deep within him.

Whatever it was, she felt she was standing in the middle of another storm. Electricity sparked and sizzled between them.

She should move away from him but her legs wouldn't cooperate. His lips touched hers. Searching. Asking. Her arms went around him and their bodies radiated heat. She trembled as every nerve within her came alive. His mouth explored hers, awakening every nerve ending.

His hands ran up and down her body, then he pulled her even closer and she felt every muscle on him. A fiery craving spread through her as her arms went around his neck and her fingers played with the still-wet tendrils of his hair.

"You're so damn irresistible," he whispered.

Heavy approaching footsteps ended the moment abruptly. They swiftly moved apart as Chet walked in. The kiss was so unexpected she hadn't considered that there was no door. The room just opened to the hallway.

The foreman looked from one to the other. "Just checking in before leaving. Everything looks good in the stables. The kids did a great job...and I'm heading home unless there's something you need. Didn't mean to interrupt."

"You didn't," Reese replied easily. "I just asked Mrs. MacInnes to stay a few days and fill in for Sandra. She seems to have a knack for computers."

"Good idea," Chet said to Lauren as if he hadn't noticed how close she and Reese were. "Turn this guy loose on a computer, and something bad happens within minutes. I can't say I'm much better. Well, I'm off to bed." He turned red then.

Reese chuckled. "Good night," he said, obviously dismissing him. "Say hello to your wife for me."

"She's probably not all that happy with you right now for keeping me so long." He turned to Lauren. "And a good-night to you, Mrs. MacInnes," he added as he turned and walked swiftly away.

Reese stepped back farther. "I keep forgetting there's not a door here. There's usually just the three of us, and Sally and Nathan usually stay in the back wing." His hand went to her shoulder. "Chet won't say anything."

Part of her had been relieved when Chet entered, while another less cautious part of her brain resented it. This—whatever "this" was—was moving so fast. Maybe too fast. He was exhausted. Truth be told, she was, as well. They were both susceptible to runaway feelings.

She grabbed at the thought as if it was a lifeline even

though her heart was still speeding. She hastily drove the subject into another lane. "Sally said you and Chet grew up together."

"We did. Chet's father was my father's foreman. Both thought the ranch gave them God-like authority, like in the old Western movies. Chet and I grew up together, learned to ride together. When he finished high school, he went to work at the ranch, and I went to college.

"It's a long story," he continued, "but when my father was badly injured, Chet's father tried to wrest control of the ranch. I was at college and Sally was only fourteen.

"I came home. My father wasn't the same after the accident. Half the time he didn't know where he was, and he now had a physical disability. There was no one on the ranch I could trust, certainly not Chet's father, and he'd hired most of the employees. He thought he would be running Eagles' Roost after my father's accident. It wouldn't have lasted long if he had gained control," he added. "The ranch was already in trouble. He was stealing cattle, inflating cattle counts for loans, and couldn't keep ranch hands more than a month or so.

"He claimed in court that my father had made him half owner and designated him to operate the ranch. He had a paper with a signature. Chet knew it was fraudulent. He also knew what would happen to the ranch if his father succeeded. It would have been broken up and sold. He loves this valley as much as I do.

"When it was all over," Reese continued, "I fired his father but, because of Chet, with a healthy payment, and asked Chet to stay as my right hand. He's the brother I've never had. Sally feels the same about him. I'm not telling you anything private. It was all over the Colorado newspapers twenty-two ago."

"I knew I liked him. I just didn't know why," Lauren said. "What happened to his father?"

"He left, became foreman of a ranch in Texas and was fired. Chet gave him money until he died of a heart attack."

She had so many other questions to ask. She wanted to know if he'd ever married, ever been in love. He seemed so self-contained.

But instead, she played with his hand. It was strong, calloused. "That kiss…that was the first since Dane."

"What do you think he would want for you?" Reese asked gently.

She thought about it, but then she knew. "He would want me to be happy. You two have a lot in common. He was disowned by his father because he joined the air force instead of the family business, and he loved us especially hard because there was no one else to share his love with."

"I doubt that was the only reason," he said.

"No. I shouldn't have said it like that. It's just he had so much love bottled up inside. It was just so damn unfair…a drunk driver after he'd survived so many missions. I don't know if either Julie or I can stand pain like that again."

He wrapped his arms around her. "I think you can handle anything, including rampaging elephants."

She felt his warmth and strength flow through her. She was falling in love and was amazed at how quickly it had happened. It had been so different with Dane. It had developed over years, not days or weeks.

How could she believe in it when she'd only known him for such a short time?

"Tell me about Dane, or is it too difficult?" he asked

as he led her over to the sofa. He gently pulled her down and put his arms around her as he waited for an answer.

"Dane came from a family, a wealthy one. He was the firstborn son and was raised from birth to run the family's business, a large financial firm in the Northeast. Problem was he hated everything to do with his father's firm and the fancy schools he attended.

"Like me, he looked up one day and watched a plane cross the sky," she said softly. "And he knew that was where he belonged."

He nodded, his hand grasping hers as she continued, "He quit college, joined the air force as an enlisted man and worked his way up, and that's extremely difficult in the air force. Nearly all pilots come out of the academy. Anyway, his family cut him off cold. Never spoke to him again, never acknowledged him. Not even Julie.

"I don't mind," she said. "Who wants contact with a family like that? But Julie does. She was the only one of her friends who had no relatives other than her father and myself. Her adored father died. There's no one but me left. That scares her."

"I can understand that. Poor kid."

Lauren nestled in his arms.

"Can I ask you something?" she said.

"Sure."

"Why do Sally and Nathan have different last names?" She'd heard the boy referred to as Nathan Howard.

Reese was silent for a moment. "It's really no secret," he said. "My father treated her terribly. He took his frustration over his situation out on her. She disappeared after graduating from high school, fell in love— or thought she did—with someone who thought she had money. She married him, and he came to me for money."

He paused, then went on, "I knew it was just the beginning, and that he was mistreating her just as Dad had. When I wouldn't give it to him and urged her to divorce him, he beat her. Badly. I found him, gave him a taste of his own medicine and told him what I would do if I ever saw him again. He believed me.

"She found out she was pregnant soon after he left. She didn't want her son to have his name and refused to put it on the birth certificate, said she didn't know it. He became Nathan Howard... She's considered taking her maiden name back."

"What about the father?"

"He was long gone by then. When I did a search later, I discovered he'd been killed in a fight. No surprise there."

"Does Nathan know what happened?"

"Yes. Everyone in town pretty much knew when she turned up pregnant here. It's next to impossible to keep secrets in this valley. We told Nathan when he heard the rumors. He had a hard time at first, but the horses, and Leo, helped a lot. So does music."

"How did Sally become a physical therapist?"

"She's a lot like you. She needs to be useful. When Nathan started school, she went to the university and got her PT degree. Betty looked after Nathan during the week and Sally returned on weekends. She's still a traveling PT except during these few weeks of our Junior Rancher program. But she chooses her jobs for only short periods of time."

Lauren's respect for Sally jumped even higher. She'd overcome a lot and became her own person, a strong one.

After a moment, Reese continued, "Nathan is like a

son to me and I'm glad he has the Howard name. He's a good kid."

"I've noticed."

She snuggled deeper into his arms.

"Are we safe here now?"

"Now that Chet has gone, I think so. The kids are in bed. Sally always stays in the other wing of the house, as does Nathan. They're both occupied now." He paused, then added softly, "I didn't mean for that kiss to happen," he said. "But I'm glad it did."

"I know," she whispered. "Me, too."

"Something has been stirring between us since we met," Reese said.

"It complicates things. Especially my staying here," she pointed out.

"I wasn't just making a job up. I do need someone who understands computers while Sandra is gone."

She nodded. He was always direct. It was one of the things she liked about him. One of the many things. She looked into those dark eyes and knew an aching need deep inside. She knew what she should do. Walk away. Now.

She also knew what she *wanted* to do. Stay and see where this…undeniable attraction led them. But there was her daughter to consider. If Chet noticed something, so would Julie. She didn't think her daughter would react well. She was so protective of her dad.

But Lauren wanted to stay. She wanted to ride up into the mountains and she wanted to explore the ranch and she wanted, darn it, to feel the warmth of Reese's arms. It felt so natural. She wasn't ready to throw something this fine away.

"I have to go back to Covenant Falls in the morning,"

she said softly. "I'm in dire need of clothing, and it's all there. I have a riding lesson scheduled, as well."

He leaned his head down and kissed the top of her nose. "Heaven forbid," he said, "that you miss a riding lesson a hundred and fifty miles away. Have you noticed we have a few instructors here, myself included?"

"I hear they're a very demanding group," she retorted.

"It depends on the rider. And you have a very fetching nose. Has anyone told you that before?"

She burst out laughing. "I can honestly say they have not," she responded as she traced a pattern on his hand. His fingers were long and calloused. They were obviously newly washed but they reminded her of what a long two days he'd had. "You should go to bed," she pointed out.

"You're right, and so should you, but this is a conversation I want to resume."

"My nose isn't that interesting."

"Everything about you is intriguing," he replied. He paused, then added, "You will stay for a while?"

"How can I say no after such a compliment to my nose, but I do have to go to Covenant Falls tomorrow."

"You can borrow some clothes from Sally," he suggested.

"I need my own. I just bought some fancy new jeans that are sitting in a suitcase. And some boots. I came for a picnic only."

"And you had an adventure instead, and I discovered a woman of many talents. Counterfeit money. Poker. Subterfuge."

"Don't forget computer guru."

"Ah, the most important of all. Does that mean you'll stay?"

"After I drive to Covenant Falls and pick up my belongings." She hesitated, then added, "At least for a few days. Any longer depends on how Julie responds to the idea."

His arms tightened around her again. "When will you be back?"

"I'll leave around seven in the morning," she said. "I have a riding lesson at twelve. I don't want to cancel it this late. Luke has a pretty busy schedule. I'll stay overnight and be back the next morning."

He brushed back a wayward curl that fell over her eyes. "That's good. I want to show you something then."

"What?"

"I can't really explain it, but you'll like it."

"About staying after Thursday…"

He waited for her to continue.

"I'll have to talk to Julie, see whether it's okay with her. Coming here was all for her. I don't want to bust in and ruin it for her."

"I understand that." He leaned down and kissed her again, this time lightly. "But selfishly, I want you to stay. You brighten this ranch, not only for me but everyone else, too. You've turned us into a family rather than a program."

She was stunned and touched at the words. Mist started to blind her eyes. She knew if she stayed a moment longer, she would be in his arms again, and that wouldn't solve anything.

She nodded. "Good night" was all she could say as she barely managed to stand and take the steps that would propel her toward her room.

Chapter 11

Lauren woke to sun pouring through her window.

The bed was comfortable, the large colorful quilt was soft and cozy, and she didn't want to get up. She immediately thought about Reese and the kiss last night and her response to it.

She also felt guilty and disloyal. It had been less than two years since Dane died. How could she feel so drawn to another man? How could she possibly stay here when every meeting between Reese and herself erupted into internal fireworks? There was no way they could keep their attraction private.

The drive today might give her some perspective. She had none at the moment. She just wanted to feel his arms around her again. The word *family* kept creeping into her thoughts. The ranch had felt like a family last night: one big boisterous family. It was something she'd always wanted.

She got up, wrapped a towel around herself and looked out the window. Even after the late night, the ranch was bustling. She went into the bathroom and looked at her clothes with distaste. They smelled like horse. She'd thought about washing them last night but she knew they wouldn't dry in time.

This was Tuesday. She'd first driven up to Eagles' Roost a week ago Sunday. The world—at least her world—had changed within that time. She hadn't thought she could love again, especially this soon. She feared she was reaching that point.

It was much too early to think—or feel—in those terms. She'd never believed in love at first sight, or first day or even first week.

She picked over every word he'd said, trying to find a clue to his past romance, or romances. Had he married? If so, there was no evidence of it. She could ask Sally but no, she couldn't. No one had said anything. Asking would invite questions she couldn't answer. She could look him up on the internet, but that seemed an invasion.

She took a cold shower, then a hot shower and washed her hair with the care package Sally had given her last night. She was wrapped in a towel when a knock came at the door. She opened it and peeked out.

Her daughter stood there with a pile of clothes in her hands. "Hi, Mom," she said.

It was the cheeriest "hi, Mom" she'd heard in the past sixteen months, and Lauren's heart soared.

"From Sally," Julie continued. "She got your clothes last night and washed them. She said hers were too large. They were. You looked kind of funny. They were also rather messy after stomping around in the stable."

Relief flooded Lauren as she accepted the clothes.

"Well, thank you. How she finds time to do everything is beyond my comprehension, but I'm grateful. I'm going back to Covenant Falls this morning. My luggage is there. I'd planned on being here one afternoon, not two and a half days."

"But you *are* coming back?" Julie pleaded. "That was so much fun last night."

Lauren raised her eyebrows. "Cleaning stalls? Fun?"

"Yeah. We made a game out of it."

"I think you did a fantastic job," Lauren said honestly as she clutched her towel. "All of you. You certainly surprised the ranch hands."

"I kinda like Nathan," Julie blurted out as if she couldn't hold it in any longer.

Warning bells went off in Lauren's head. "Does he *kinda* like you?"

"I don't know for sure, but maybe."

"He's older than you."

"Just eighteen months. I'm fifteen and he just turned seventeen."

"That's a lot of difference at your age and you're only here for two and a half more weeks," Lauren said. *Listen to yourself and heed.*

Julie looked cautious. "I know."

"I want to ask you something," Lauren said.

"What?" Julie asked cautiously.

Lauren took a deep breath, then said, "Mr. Howard and Sally have asked me to stay this week and help with some computer problems. Is that okay with you?"

Julie hesitated just long enough to ring more warning bells in her head. The last thing she wanted to do was alienate her daughter. She couldn't forget Dane's sadness that came from losing his family.

But then, Julie grinned. "It's okay. Jenny and the boys really like you. They're jealous I have a mom they can have fun with."

It wasn't exactly the roaring approval she'd hoped for, but then Julie was a teenager. She took the okay as consent.

"Then I'll try it," Lauren said. "I'll be back in the morning. I want to be here for the recognition ceremony. I'm sorry the other parents can't. You guys have worked so hard."

"There's whispers there will be a surprise," Julie said. "Because of last night."

"Then I'll definitely make it back." She tested another idea. "It's not a bad drive. It's scenic, and I can't wait for you to visit Covenant Falls. You'll love it. I've been thinking that maybe we can look at property around here. You could have a horse here. Unless you want to stay in San Antonio."

Julie looked uncertain. "I don't know. I haven't thought about it. Dad loved...Texas."

He loved it because he flew there. But Lauren didn't want to say that. She changed the subject back to the present. "Whatever we do it will be a joint decision. Think about it."

"How long will you be staying at the ranch?" Julie asked.

"Depends on when their business manager returns. They expect her back within a week."

"You know I'm seeing a whole new mom here," her daughter said. "Especially Monday. I never thought I would see you sweeping out a stall."

"I'm the same one, sweetie," Lauren replied.

"I always...felt you liked flying better than anything."

"Oh, Julie, I'm sorry. That's never been true. You've always been first with me."

Julie ducked her head. "I knew that when you resigned your commission." She smiled. "But I'm really glad you're staying, and you looked super good on that horse."

"Thank you, daughter." She reached over and hugged Julie.

"Are you leaving now?"

"Right after breakfast," Lauren said.

"I'm glad you stayed here the last two nights," Julie said. "Thanks for insisting that I come here."

"Did I insist?"

"Pretty much," Julie replied with a smile.

"Want to have breakfast with me before I leave?"

"I already ate, and it's time to feed Snowflake." She gave Lauren another quick hug and moved faster than Lauren had noticed before. Lauren followed her out the door and watched as Julie started down the stairs. She wasn't using the crutches and she was walking better with a brace. She'd worked just as hard as anyone last night.

Lauren looked at the mound of clothes, then got dressed.

She grabbed her purse and keys and went down to the kitchen. Pancakes were on the menu, along with fried eggs, bacon, thick slices of ham and fried potatoes.

Betty greeted her. "Good morning," she said. "Thanks for all your help last night."

"Believe it or not, it was fun," Lauren said. "It feels good to be useful again. Where's Sally? I wanted to thank her for the clean clothes."

"She's grabbing a few hours of sleep."

"What about you?"

"I'll get mine this afternoon. And I did get some sleep last night."

"Everyone else gone?"

"Some of the ranch hands left at dawn," Betty said. "They're still looking for strays and putting fences together at the new pasture. Others are sleeping. The riding instructor arrived and will take care of the riding sessions today. Reese will be back in time for the mustang visits."

"Reese went with them this morning?"

"He did. That man never stops."

"Doesn't seem like anyone on the ranch ever stops," Lauren observed. She helped herself to several pancakes. She figured she worked it off in advance last night. She added bacon, a slice of ham and some fried potatoes.

"I like a good appetite," Betty said.

"Good, because I'm driving to Covenant Falls today to pick up my luggage. I'll be back tomorrow to start working on the computer."

"Thank the Good Lord," Betty exclaimed. "Reese is a temperate man until it comes to that machine and it doesn't work, which is most of the time he uses it. To tell you the truth, he resents anything he can't do well. And since he does most things well, he takes his ire out on the few he doesn't."

Lauren had difficulty believing that. Reese seemed to be the most even-tempered man she'd ever met. "What about Nathan?"

"Nathan's better than Reese, but he's no computer genius, either. His life is horses and music. I'm not sure yet which will win out."

Lauren smiled. "It would be downright unfair if they

were good at everything. There would be nothing left for us mortals to do."

Betty laughed.

Lauren finished her breakfast. "Thanks, Betty. I'm off."

Reese pulled a calf out of muddy water and balanced him on the front of the saddle. He'd brought three of the ranch hands to find any of the animals they'd missed last night in the dark.

He hadn't waited this morning to talk to Lauren. He wanted to get out and pick up stragglers from last night. And he didn't want to give her an opportunity to change her mind about staying.

He should have told her about his wife, but the pain was still deep and he hadn't wanted to scare her off, although he doubted she scared easily. Anyone who piloted jets full of ammunition wouldn't be easily scared. When his cousin Patti first mentioned Julie as a possible prospect for the program he was dubious about her being a good fit. Certainly, an air force major and widow of a colonel had resources that most of the kids in the program didn't.

Lauren had been a surprise in many ways. He hadn't wanted to like her when he first saw her with her indignant "why weren't you here?" look. But her interest in mustangs started to temper his feelings, and when she leaned down to greet Leo by scratching him in all his favorite places, he started wondering what other surprises awaited him.

More than he'd bargained for.

And now he'd lowered himself to using the computer to keep her here. He wasn't quite as bad as he portrayed himself, but if he couldn't do something well, he damn well didn't want to do it at all. It was one of his admitted failings, and everyone on the ranch had heard him swearing at the damn thing.

Maybe it was finally proving its worth.

He reached the other cowhands and signaled, "Let's go home."

As soon as she reached Covenant Falls, Lauren wanted to turn around and return to Eagles' Roost, even as she wondered how she could become attached to a place so quickly. Or to a man so deeply.

After retrieving her suitcase, the only commitment she had here was the riding lesson. She could do that and get back before dark.

She thought she needed time to consider everything that had happened over the past few days, that maybe she could do so more logically away from Eagles' Roost. But she quickly decided she could do that on the ride back. Besides, this was the day her daughter was meeting her mustang.

She checked her watch. Her riding appointment was at twelve, an hour from now.

Jimmy, the same desk clerk who had greeted her when she arrived a week ago, was on duty.

"Happy to see you again, Mrs. MacInnes. When we heard about the trouble at Eagles' Roost, we left your room as it was. No charge for the extra days. We haven't needed the room and we understand floods around here. Do you still have the key or do you need a new one?"

"I have it, thanks, but I'm just staying until around 1:00 p.m. I'll be vacating the room then."

"I hope there's no problem."

"No, everything has been lovely. Better than that, really. It's been perfect. I'm staying at the Eagles' Roost Ranch for a few days."

"Mr. Howard often stays here," he said. "He's one of our favorite guests. Is there anything we can do for you?" he added.

"No, thank you."

"I can heat up some rolls for you," he offered.

She groaned. "I had a huge breakfast this morning, but thanks."

She went to her room.

It was exactly as she'd left it, except the bed was made and the bathroom was spotless. She opened her small laptop and went online. She hadn't taken it to Eagles' Roost. She'd been too much in a hurry to get there and had overlooked it. That was a first for her.

Eagles' Roost, she decided, had placed a spell on her.

Maybe it was a good spell. She felt alive, truly alive, for the first time since Dane died. It wasn't only Reese, although he was a big part of it; it was also the pleasure of seeing her daughter find something she loved as much as running. She didn't know how she would manage it but she was determined to give her daughter that horse. And a dog.

The phone rang. "Hi," Reese said. His deep voice warmed her. "Just wanted to make sure you made it okay. Some roads are still pretty bad."

"No problems on this one," she said as she pictured him in her mind. He would be in jeans, maybe in a dark blue shirt with his worn boots and worn cowboy hat. Probably leaning over the fence and staring at the mustangs.

"It's a long drive."

"It's nothing compared to some of the flights I've piloted," she said. "It's good thinking time."

"Reach any conclusions?"

"As a matter of fact, I have," she said. "I've been thinking about your computer on the way here," she added, trying to keep amusement from her voice. "I think maybe if you named it something warm and fuzzy, like Maggie, it would respond better. I think it senses your hostility."

There was a silence, then a chuckle. "Maybe I better find another computer fixer."

"Then she would really throw a tantrum."

"I can't let that happen," he replied. "Maggie it is, and I'll give all the credit to you." He paused, then added, "I miss you already," he said, the laughter gone.

"I'm heading out to my riding lesson."

"You know there's a few riding instructors around here," he said.

"But they're already booked up to capacity," she retorted, then added seriously, "I don't want to compete with my daughter. Eagles' Roost is meant to be *her* world. I don't want to break into it. If I'm there, I want to be in the background. I don't want to take up teaching time. I *do* want to see my daughter taming a mustang.

"And," she added, "Luke and I understand each other," she continued, trying her best to explain to herself as well as to him. "Student and teacher. However, I am not averse to private instruction from time to time."

"I'll see if someone can provide it."

"How is Julie?"

"She met her mustang this morning. She has the black mare and named her Midnight. The selections were made by picking names from a box. I didn't want anything to do with it."

"Chicken!"

"When it comes to choosing mustangs for kids, yeah, I'm a chicken. As for Julie, she's reading a story to Midnight now. She's about eight feet away from her and the mare is listening. Julie has a great voice for this. Calm. Soothing. She is definitely your daughter," he added. "She's becoming a regular little equestrian."

"I'm soothing? No one has ever called me that before... Has she said anything to you about her leg?"

"She's taking off her brace more. Is that okay?"

"Now that the foot is responding, she needs to work on improving the movement. But while on a horse, I worry that the foot might get twisted in some way so I think it's wise to use the brace while riding."

"Okay," he said. "Still staying until tomorrow?"

"No, I decided to head back after the lesson."

"Great. Enjoy and drive safely." He hung up.

She glanced at her watch. She had thirty minutes before the lesson. She chose one of the new pairs of jeans and a green-and-white-checkered shirt, brushed her hair back and pulled on her boots.

She packed everything else into her suitcase. She'd had to buy a new one for the trip. She hadn't used anything but duffels for more years than she wanted to count. She stopped to consider that, nostalgia knocking at her mental door.

When everything was in the car, she checked out, thanked Jimmy for everything and drove to Luke's ranch.

"You've improved," he said when she cantered around

the circle and pulled up neatly when he gave the signal. "You've had some practice."

"Not much," she replied, "but some, and I have to cancel tomorrow's lesson. I'm returning to the ranch today."

He nodded. "You have a new sparkle in your eyes. Mountain air seems to suit you."

"It does."

"Might you be staying longer than you expected?"

"I'm not sure."

"I think you are," he said with a twinkle. "Reese?"

She nodded. It was impossible to lie to him.

Luke nodded. "He's one of the good guys. You two are suited for each other if I've ever seen it. You're quiet on the outside and full of heart inside."

"It's been such a short time," she protested as she dismounted and led the horse to the stable.

"When you know, you know," he said. "I took one look at a girl barrel racing at a rodeo one evening and knew I was going to marry her. She thought I was crazy when we met, and I told her that. We've been married now for more than forty years and I love her more each day." He paused. "Don't let it get away from you."

She stretched up and kissed him on the cheek. "Thank you."

He just nodded and turned away.

She glanced at her watch as she hurried back to the car. It was just twelve thirty. She had just enough time for one last stop before heading back to the ranch...

Otis Davies was tinkering again, this time with the two-seater trainer.

"Didn't know if I would see you again," he said when she reached him.

"Oh, I think you knew."

"Mebbe." He smiled.

"I might be staying in the area longer than I thought," she said.

"I heard you were at Eagles' Roost up the road," he commented.

"My daughter's there."

"Heard that, too," he said.

She just shook her head. She should have known.

"Are you interested in my proposal?" he prompted.

"I don't know," she replied. "Not freight. I have a pretty good idea when you make those flights. Storms. Snow. When roads are blocked. I have a fifteen-year-old daughter going on sixteen who lost her father. I can't take those risks anymore."

"But...?" he finished for her.

"Teaching. You mentioned that. I could be interested." She hurried on, "I don't even know where I'll be or how long, but I know I love this area and would like to stay around here or farther up in the mountains. I'm thinking maybe classes one or two days a week if you think there would be any demand."

"Interesting," he said. "You could talk to the high schools in the area... I think they would swarm over here. I'm just an old coot."

"Remember, I learned from an old coot," she said. "I just wanted to feel you out," she said. "I'm not sure any of it is possible. I might even be leaving the area in a few weeks. It might be a wild, impossible idea but..."

"You're doing your prep work just in case?"

"Right."

"Nothing would pleasure me more than having this place fill with people again. But isn't it a long way from where you're staying now?"

She shrugged. "A few hours once or twice a week, but I don't know how long I'll be there. I do know I like this part of the country. I'm just thinking about possibilities now."

He nodded and thrust out his hand. "I hope it works out."

Wheels were turning in her head as she headed for Eagles' Roost. She wasn't even sure *why* she just did what she did. She might be leaving in a few weeks.

It was just that pesky compulsion to figure all angles of any possible move, no matter how impossible it seemed.

She didn't think Julie would object to leaving Texas. She'd only lived in San Antonio a few months after Lauren's transfer to Lackland. The rest of the time had been mostly in military hospitals.

But she might never convince her daughter that flying again was safer than driving a car.

All she knew was she wanted to protect her daughter first and have a goal of her own, small as it might be.

She arrived back at the ranch in time to see her daughter standing in front of the large black horse in one of the four pens outside the mustang stable. Soft music came from her small computer and she was reading from her e-reader. The horse was not fooled. She was on alert. Lauren knew the signs now.

Reese and Robin were standing farther away. Watching. Not moving.

Some other hands were watching, as well.

Reese nodded to Julie.

Julie stepped toward the pen as Reese joined her and together they approached the horse. Reese held out a carrot to her. The horse snorted and backed up. He then gave the carrot to Julie and backed away. "Put it on the railing," he directed her. Julie did as told, then backed up. The horse waited until they retreated, then approached, sniffed the carrot and took it.

Reese nodded his approval. "We'll offer the carrot again later today and twice tomorrow. She'll start associating the carrot with you."

The two of them came over to Lauren, and a broad grin stretched over Julie's face.

"Julie did great," Reese praised, "although I'm not sure Midnight is the most cheerful choice for a black horse."

"I doubt if the horse cares," Lauren replied.

Robin, who'd been standing with them, laughed. "She doesn't," she said. "I'm really proud of Julie. She's fearless."

"That's what scares me," Lauren replied.

"She apparently takes after her mom," Reese said.

"That scares *me* even more." Lauren hugged Julie. "You're becoming a fine horsewoman. I'm sorry I wasn't here to watch everything."

"It's boring," Julie said. "Not to me because I'm talking to her, but it would be to someone watching."

"I wanted to be here when you had your first visit with the mustang." Lauren said. "I'm going to take my luggage inside," she said. "I'll see you at dinner."

As she walked toward the house, she wondered about Julie's lack of enthusiasm this morning when she announced she would be staying. Was she having second thoughts about her mother staying at the house or had she heard something linking her with Reese?

Nathan was coming out of the house when he saw her. "Can I help you, Mrs. MacInnes?"

"Sure. I would appreciate it."

He led the way to her room and put the luggage down. "That was a pretty neat thing you did last night. The guys all appreciated it."

"It was the kids," she insisted. *Was it only last night?*

He chuckled. "I heard you had a trip today?"

"To Covenant Falls and back."

"That *is* long," he said. "Betty said supper will be at six thirty in the dining room. There's nothing afterward. I think everyone is pretty exhausted today."

"Did you get all the cattle safely away?"

"Yes, ma'am. They'll stay up in the high pasture now for two months, then we'll bring them back when the weather starts getting cold. We can protect them better here and it's easier to provide feed if they need it." He started to leave.

"I hear you're a musician."

"I like to play music. Not sure that qualifies me as a musician."

"I would like to hear you."

"There will be the celebration tomorrow night. I think Uncle Reese has some special plans for it. He's asked me to sing a few songs."

"I look forward to it."

He went to the door. "Julie's doing really good in her riding. Even with the brace, she's one of the best we've had since Uncle Reese started the program. She said she won't need it much longer."

"She's right. We're just being cautious now."

"That's…good. I heard she used to run."

"She did. That's what is so helpful about this program. She's competitive, she likes to test herself and she hasn't been able to do that for a long time. The only thing I fear now is that she tries to do too much, especially with one of the mustangs."

"We'll watch her. Thanks for telling me."

"Thank you," she said.

After he left, she unpacked her suitcase, then checked her watch. It was nearly time for supper. She chose a new pair of jeans and a tan shirt and went downstairs to the dining room. There were just five of them: Betty, Sally, Chet and Ann, and herself.

"There's usually more of us," Sally said. "Reese is catching up on some sleep. Nathan decided to eat with the teens—he's more involved this year than before—and we usually have some visiting instructors but the storm has sent everything off-kilter."

Betty explained, "The teens eat at the table in the kitchen. We gave them a choice, and they settled on the kitchen at night so they can talk about us while we talk about them. The morning is catch as you can. There's a buffet in the dining room. Everyone has a different time schedule. Lunch is pretty much the same."

"Except for *this* Saturday," Chet said. "That will be interesting."

"Have the teens said anything about the menu?" she asked.

"I think they made Betty take a vow of silence," Sally replied. "How was your trip?"

The attention turned to Lauren. "Good. The riding lesson was great and now I have my clothes with me."

"Well, we're happy you're joining us," Sally said. "The evildoer might complain but that's to be expected."

"The evildoer?" she asked.

"The computer. Reese swears it's alive and targets him. The name changes according to his current frustration. Sometimes it's the monster, sometimes the evildoer. He says now there's a new sheriff in town and you're it."

She raised her eyebrows in mock horror. "*I'm* the sheriff? I already suggested he take a friendlier tact. Like calling her Maggie."

"How did he take that?"

"I'm not entirely sure," she replied. "He was kinda silent when I mentioned it."

"I bet." Chet chuckled.

The discussion turned to schedules being changed because of the rain. The weather report predicted clear skies the rest of the week. "Of course, that's what they said last week," Sally quipped.

When they finished, most of them headed for their beds as a result of the lingering effects of the storm. When Lauren went to check on Julie, Sally mentioned both girls had gone to bed early.

Lauren was tired as well, but she was also restless. She went outside. The mustangs were in their pens. Each pen was about twice the size of a stall and had its own water and feed bucket. She heard a loud braying of protest and went toward the sound.

"Noisy little beast, isn't he?" Reese said from behind her.

She spun around. "At least he doesn't sneak up on people and scare them to death."

"I just fed him. He was alone in the stable. He couldn't get into the pens with his friends. Well, maybe *friends* isn't the word for it. More like his victims. He likes to terrorize them. I didn't mean to scare you."

"You weren't at dinner."

"I caught an hour's sleep. I imagine you know what that's like."

She smiled, remembering. All pilots slept with one eye open. They never knew when or where they would be sent next. They slept when they could. "Yeah, I do."

"Want to go for a ride?"

"At night?"

"Sure. It's one of the best times. We're almost at full moon tonight."

"Yes," she said, "I would, but you didn't have dinner."

"I just happen to know where the fridge is."

"I guess you do," she said with a smile.

"I also know where some horses are."

"Did you know I would be out here?"

"No, but I hoped."

"Why?"

"Because I want you to see something."

"And you don't think anyone will see us tonight?"

He chuckled. "I think nearly everyone is exhausted after last night and should be in bed with the exception of a few I can trust."

"Okay, where are we going?"

"A favorite place of mine. It's a short ride."

He led her into the main stable and went down the aisle until he stopped at a stall.

"Max is already saddled," she observed.

"I was going for a ride," he said. "It's a beautiful night. It often is after a storm. Everything is cleansed."

"I noticed," she answered softly. "Who am I riding?"

"I took a chance and saddled Lady."

"Good. I like her."

He led both horses out and gave Lauren a boost into

the saddle. They walked out and turned in the direction they had taken on their prior ride.

He was right. The moon was huge with only a sliver hidden behind the mountains. The light bounced off the snowcapped mountains to the west and spread its glow over the valley. It was spectacular. He stopped and looked at her.

"You're right," she said. "It's beautiful."

"It's supposed to be clear again tomorrow night. I'm thinking about bringing the kids here for the celebration."

"I think you should," she said. "It's fantastic. What would you have done had I not come down?"

"Come anyway. I wanted to see if it might work tomorrow night."

"Where are we going now?" she asked.

"Not far."

They were going on the same trail they took Sunday, then he turned off on another one until they came to a spring. She slipped down before he could reach her. He took her hand and led her to what looked like a small cemetery protected by a wrought iron fence. He led her inside.

He stopped at the smallest marker. "Many of the Howards are buried here," he said, "including the founder and my father." His hand tightened around hers. "There's no one under the smallest one," he said. "Only a memory. A son that never lived.

"I brought you here because something is happening between us and I want you to know the dangers of living here. I married when I was twenty-eight. Cara was from Denver, an executive with a high-tech firm. My father had died a year earlier and I was ready to start a family.

"She was everything I thought I wanted. Smart. Funny. Loving," he added, a sad note in his voice.

"We started having problems after the first year. A ranch sounded romantic to her but the reality was far different from what she imagined. Cara couldn't find friends with common interests. The ranch took most of my time and what money we had. It had been heavily in debt when I inherited it. In the next few years, cattle prices were down and feed prices up. Even after eight years, we were still rebuilding the stock that had been decimated.

"Cara resented sharing a house with Sally. That's when I divided the house the way I did. I thought it would give her the privacy she wanted, and still be home for Sally and Nathan. I made it clear I wasn't going to abandon them. It was their home as much as mine.

"We tried. We both did. I tried taking her on trips, but then there was always an emergency and we had to come back. By the fourth year we were talking divorce. What love we had was damaged by arguments and demands. We'd decided on a divorce a month before learning she was pregnant. We agreed we would try again."

He stopped, and Lauren sensed something very painful was coming. After a short pause, he continued, "To make it short, the baby came early during a snowstorm and I couldn't get my wife to a hospital in time to save him. The doctors thought that if we had, he might have lived.

"His name was going to be Adam." There was a world of hurt when Reese said the name.

"We were both devastated. Cara asked for a divorce and by then I knew it wasn't worth another try. The baby would always be between us. She buried Adam in Denver. I put a stone here in our family cemetery. He deserved acknowledgment that he existed, even for a very short period of time."

Mist clouded her eyes. Her heart cried for him. She held on to his hand tightly as he fell into silence.

He broke the quiet several minutes later. "I've avoided serious relationships since. I always felt like I destroyed her life. I love this land," he said, "but it's not for everyone."

"Did she ever remarry?"

"I received an invitation to the wedding five years later."

"Then you *didn't* ruin her life."

"I hope not."

"And is Adam the reason for your program?"

"Not consciously. I just heard about the need from friends in Covenant Falls, and realized I had the space and the horses. Sally is a physical therapist and worked hard to get there, but she spends so much time looking after Nathan and me she doesn't have much time to take assignments.

"And then I have friends who train horses and teach riding. We have a retired psychologist neighbor friend in town who helped develop the program. I wanted to single out emotionally troubled or physically handicapped children of veterans who'd died in combat."

"And now," she said, "you're warning off all potential women friends?"

"That sounds…"

"Very self-protective."

He grinned suddenly. "Are you always so blunt?"

"I'm afraid so. When I lost Dane, I thought I would never marry again. It hurt too damn much when I lost him. He was a good guy. A real good one despite his background."

"Tell me more about him. Or is it too painful?"

"No. We met in advanced training and disliked each other on sight. I came out of a poor background where we scrambled for everything. He had the Ivy League manners and speech.

"I thought he was a snob, and he didn't like me any better. And we were competitors." She grinned at the memory. "Were we ever competitors!

"I'm not sure when everything changed. It started one night when we were all drinking. Someone asked him about his family. He said he didn't have one. It was the way he said it that hit me at the gut level. Over the next weeks I coaxed the story from him. His family never talked to him again after he joined the air force.

"They didn't even contact us after I tried to notify them of Dane's death. They couldn't care less about their granddaughter. That's what continues to hurt me. Julie doesn't understand."

"That's a hell of a lot for a kid," he said. He took her hands in his. "I'm so sorry. But she has you, and that's a hell of a lot, too."

"It hasn't been enough. Until, maybe, now. She's making friends. She's talking to me a little. She loves the horse and feels good about herself again. I can see the pride on her face when she canters, and the intensity with which she read to Midnight. I'm getting my Julie back and I can't tell you how much that means to me."

He listened intently. "She really has been through hell. Both of you."

"It's been nearly a year and a half, and this week is

the first time I've seen her smile, really smile, since the accident."

He closed his eyes and to her amazement, she thought she saw a tear. It might have been the reflective moonlight. Then he put his arms around her and just held her.

"I'm so sorry."

"She's so much better in the short time she's been here. It helps that she can share with other kids who have gone through similar traumas, that she's not alone." She turned around and faced him. "You're doing good, mister."

"A tiny little drop in an ocean," he said. "Do you want to go back to the air force? I imagine the door is still open."

"I want to keep flying but I won't go back to the air force. I can't do that to Julie. She's terrified of losing the only family member she has left."

"I get that." He stood, offered her his hand and pulled her up into his arms. "I like you a lot, Mrs. MacInnes."

The air between them was thick with emotion. His fingers stroked her cheek, then curled around her neck. Her arms went around him, his breath whispering against her lips. Then their lips met, lightly at first, then hungrily with all the heat that had been building between them. She responded with an intensity that shook her.

His hands traced her form, touching lightly, and she marveled at the wells of tenderness that accompanied the passion roaring between them. At the same time she felt a glow, a warmth that filled her so completely that she suddenly realized how lonely she had been.

The howl of a coyote separated them. She looked at him askance.

"We should go," he said. "This is their territory at night and I don't have a weapon with me." He took her hand. "A conversation to be resumed later," he said.

"I would like that," she replied softly.

He walked her over to Lady and offered his hands to boost her up into the saddle. She leaned over instead and kissed him again. "I like you," she said. "Very much."

"Back at you," he said as his hand touched a curl.

The coyote howled again.

"I think he's trying to tell us something," Reese said. He boosted her into the saddle.

"Like *go away*?" she replied as she adjusted her hands on the reins.

"I was thinking more like *get on with it*."

"I think I like your translation best," she conceded as they turned back to the house.

Chapter 12

Lauren lingered under the hot shower the next morning.

Was she really falling in love? It seemed traitorous and yet she thought Dane would approve. Dane and Reese would have liked each other. Good men, both.

Yet, she had reservations. Could she really confine herself to the ranch? Would she not look up at the sky every day and long to be there? She felt terribly sad for the loss of that baby years ago. What if it had been she who'd lost a child?

She turned off the faucet, wrapped herself in a towel and padded to the window. There were riders in the ring. She looked at her watch and was startled to see it was already past nine. She dressed quickly in a pair of jeans, one of her new shirts and her riding boots.

Lauren went down to the dining room. The room was empty and the buffet was almost gone. There were various packages of cereals, a bowl of fruit, some pastries. She headed for the coffee urn and filled a cup.

Betty appeared at the door. "Can I fry bacon and eggs for you? It would just take a jiffy."

She started to say "no, don't bother" but changed her mind. She was starving after last night's outing. "That would be great, thank you. Has everyone else eaten?"

"You are the last. Reese was the first." Betty disappeared back into the kitchen as Lauren wondered if word had leaked that she'd been out with Reese last night.

She finished breakfast quickly, thanked Betty and walked outside. Heath was talking to a mustang as Reese stood nearby. The horse, instead of scooting as far away as possible, seemed to be listening. As she approached she discovered the boy was not speaking but singing.

Reese gestured for her to come over.

As she neared, she heard an old Scottish lullaby. *Heath's good*, she mouthed to him.

"Very good. I don't think Nathan knows that. It wasn't in any of the information I had. I'm going to have to get the two together," Reese said.

"I wonder if he learned that song from his father. Maybe it was too painful for him to sing any of those songs until now. He's sharing his hurt with the horse."

Reese nodded. "You're right. The horse is responding to him quicker than any of the others and yet, like Jenny, he's been one of the quietest of the bunch."

Lauren didn't speak again until the song ended. She wanted to grab Reese's hand and share the moment in a more intimate way. Instead, she asked, "Are you going to take them out to see the moon tonight?"

He nodded. "Yep. But I'm keeping it a surprise. We'll

all have dinner at the house, then a bonfire while the ranch hands saddle the kids' horses."

"Sounds like fun," Lauren said. "I'm going to go check on Julie. She's in the ring now."

"Mary said she's doing exceptionally well, particularly since she has that brace on one side."

"I'm so proud of her and how she's fitting in."

He nodded. "I can tell she's turning into the leader of the pack. The others seem to look up to her. She really looks after Jenny."

"Anything I can help with, especially with the computer since that's why I'm here."

"Nope."

"Is there really anything wrong with the computer? Or do you just enjoy having something to complain about?"

"Well, I could tell you..."

A new voice broke in. "When he starts that 'Well, I'll tell you' business, take it with a huge grain of salt," Chet said as he waited for Reese's attention. "It's almost always a lie."

"Where did you come from?" Reese asked with mock anger.

"From doing what you asked me to do."

"That's fine. Just fine. Now, isn't there something else you need to do?"

"I think I'm leaving on that note to check on my daughter," Lauren said. She walked over to the ring and perched on the railing.

Leo followed her.

Mary Abbot, the instructor, had placed a two-foot jump in the ring. Julie cantered around the ring, then headed toward the jump, leaning forward in her saddle. Snowflake glided over the obstacle.

Lauren's stomach jumped with it. She decided it was best not to watch. Then she saw Nathan watching intently, as well. She hoped Julie wouldn't get too attached to him. She was still too young. They were miles apart and not only in interests.

Miles apart. Just like Reese and herself. What was she doing falling for someone who was the opposite of her? She and Dane were alike in so many ways. Their love of flying. Their love for their daughter. Travel. They had taken Julie all over Europe.

She continued to watch until Julie finished and took her horse inside.

Mary came over to Lauren. "She's a natural."

"She's always been very athletic."

"Have you thought about continuing her riding after she leaves here? Competitively?"

"Don't they start at an early age?"

"It helps, of course, when they start early, but she has enough natural talent to do well. She also has a competitive spirit."

"I've seen that in her running."

"I could recommend some good trainers. Depends on where you live."

"When I find that out, I'll be in touch."

"I'll be around until the end of the program," Mary said. "Reese knows how to reach me."

"I heard you did educational videos with Reese."

"Not together, but for the same company. They're trying to get him to do more videos. He has everything they're looking for—authority, experience, knowledge."

And good looks.

Lauren didn't like the seed of jealousy that was starting to bubble inside. It was none of her business anyway. Unless she got a job, they couldn't afford lessons, much less boarding, food and vet bills.

She went inside the stable where Julie was cooling off Snowflake. "She's the greatest horse, Mom. She just soared over the jump. Mary says I have real potential."

"I watched you. It was wonderful. I'm so proud of you."

"You think we can get a horse? Maybe even buy Snowflake?"

"We'll see," Lauren said. "Will you have lunch with me?"

"Sure. The other kids are envious. They think you're great."

"Great, wow. Why?"

"They like you. The poker started it. Then suggesting cleaning the stalls? A winner."

"I wouldn't think that would be a winner. They were cold, muddy and tired at the end."

"We didn't mind, and all the ranch hands loved it. They couldn't thank us enough. It was really neat, them thanking us... Anyway," she added, "you're a 'wow.'"

"I'm not quite sure what that is?"

"It's good," Julie said. She filled Snowflake's water bucket and feed box, then offered the horse a carrot. Snowflake chomped it and nuzzled her.

Julie beamed. "See, she really likes me."

Lauren thought it was more the carrot than Julie, but she let it go.

"Mr. Howard said I picked the best horse. That she had the best gait of them all, and she does. Mary agrees."

"But don't tell the others, okay? They're just as proud of their horses as you are of Snowflake."

"I wouldn't do that," her daughter said indignantly.

"How do you like the others now that more than a week has passed?"

"I really like Jenny. Tony's growing on me. He was a real jerk in the beginning, but I think he was angry. He really resents his future stepdad. I get that. I would feel the same way."

Lauren's heart dropped. "And Heath?"

"He's kind of quiet but I think it's because he hurts inside."

"I think so, too. I think he needs a friend. Someone who knows what he's going through."

"I'll try."

"You're growing into a very nice person," Lauren said. "Your dad's probably sitting up there somewhere and smiling."

She put her arm around her daughter's shoulders and they headed for the house.

Lunch was much like breakfast. Everyone came and went at their convenience. The dining room was half-full when Lauren and Julie arrived. Robin joined them. "You and Jenny both looked great today," she said. "I can honestly say that you looked better than the bunch I was with when I was a Junior Rancher at this point. That includes me."

They ate quickly. They all wanted to get back to their horses or to their time with the mustangs. When they weren't riding, they were cleaning their horses' stalls, polishing the saddle and cleaning the other equipment, or just talking to their horses.

After Julie left for her session with her mustang, Lauren decided to check "the monster," which was apparently the only thing that scared Reese Howard.

The office didn't look used since the last time she was here. She turned the computer on. It had all the safety programs and virus protection tools. She wrote an email to Patti in San Antonio and told her how well Julie was doing and that she was staying at the ranch.

The monster seemed to be working properly. She didn't think it had anything to do with a new sheriff. It had more to do with its owner's sense of humor, such as it was. It had become a collective joke.

She smiled as she turned it off.

There was no dessert with supper. After they finished dinner, the group trooped out to the picnic area in the back of the house. Several ranch hands tended a large outdoor firepit for a marshmallow roast.

The fire was already flaming. Both the kids and buddies grabbed thin metal spikes and started roasting the sweets. The night was perfect. Mild temperature. Full moon.

Reese stood when the last marshmallow was consumed. He glanced at his watch. "It's eight. We're going for a ride tonight. Get your horses and meet at the riding ring."

Everyone looked puzzled and gave each other questioning looks.

They all walked to the ring to find their horses already saddled. Lady was saddled as well and Lauren assumed the horse was meant for her. Her daughter, Jenny, Heath and Tony all looked nervous as they mounted. Reese swung up into his saddle and started in the direction he'd led her last night. There wasn't a cloud in the sky and although the moon wasn't quite as high as before, it was just as bright.

It gave enough light to easily follow the trail to a clearing under an overhanging cliff, the place Reese had brought her while she waited to see her daughter finish a riding lesson.

As it did before, the moonlight was reflected by the mountains and brightened the valley. A stream of water trickled down the cliff.

When they came to a halt, Reese maneuvered his horse in front of them. "You can dismount," he said. As the four teens dismounted and looked around curiously, ranch hands emerged from the woods around the clearing. The buddies strode to stand beside their Junior Ranchers. The other hands, along with Sally and Betty, joined the group gathered around them.

Reese dismounted, as well. "I wanted to bring you here because this is where Eagles' Roost was founded," he said. "You know the history from the information we sent you, that an eagle led the founder here.

"But," he continued, "you don't often see the valley and mountains lit by the moon like this, and I thought it was the perfect place to thank you for what you did the other night and to congratulate you all on what you've accomplished in the past week and a half. It has not been ordinary because of the flood but you're ahead of the other groups in spite of it."

He paused, then added, "You all have aced the basic horsemanship part of the program and earned our silver horseshoe pin. I was planning to do this last Sunday when your families were here but the rain interrupted that plan. I'm very proud that I can award them now. Wear them proudly because you have earned them."

He went on, "We have one more honor. And it goes to Jenny, who was judged by voters to have excelled in cleaning stalls Sunday night. Her spirit impressed everyone. Jenny, you can select the menu for all three meals next Saturday. Betty said anything goes except for pizza morning, noon and night. You can do it on your own or take suggestions."

Jenny beamed as she probably had never beamed before.

"Our ranch hands can't wait to see your menu," Reese said with a huge grin.

"We have some entertainment tonight, as well." He continued, "I heard Heath sing a song today while working with his mustang. He told me it was an old lullaby. I was carried away by it. He agreed to sing it to us tonight, and then Nathan will sing the Colorado State Song, *Where the Columbines Grow.*"

Both singers received standing ovations for their songs.

"Now it's time for hot chocolate. Pete and Terry brought some earlier in those thermos bottles in the wagon to the left of you. Don't go out of sight. You can get lost here quickly and there are coyotes around here."

Everyone clapped, then stood to congratulate Jenny, Heath, Julie and Tony.

Awakened by the clapping, Leo jumped up and wagged his tail in approval.

Chapter 13

They rode back with barely a sound. It had been a very long day and the group, including Lauren, still had to bed down their horses before going to bed.

Lauren wanted to ride next to Reese and tell him how well he handled everything. By giving everyone a pin, he eased any jealousy that might come from Jenny's win. Heath had recognition he hadn't had before and the ranch hands whom he respected clapped and hollered. He might have grown two inches in those minutes.

Reese didn't just teach riding, he made the kids believe in themselves, that they could do anything. Lauren didn't think he even realized what he was doing. It was all instinct with him. She understood now why Patti wanted Julie to come.

He made Julie believe in herself. And he was doing the same with Lauren. She'd thought flying identified her. But she was discovering she was good with people, too. She loved working with the kids and with the various staff members.

They reached the stable and had to take turns getting to the stalls. She waited behind. Some of the employees had homes to go to. She also lingered because she knew he would be the last to leave.

Then there were only two of them.

She unsaddled Lady while Reese did the same with Max six stalls down.

They walked together to the house. She didn't say anything because she would probably babble. She was happier tonight than she'd been in a long time.

"You know you did a lot of this," Reese said.

"How?" she asked, mystified.

"The way you respect everyone for who they are, the way you brought the kids together during the flood rather than sending them inside to fend for themselves. They had to work together, and they learned each had different abilities and how to meld them. This is the closest, most cohesive group we've had. I'm trying to figure out how to create a flood every year. Any ideas?"

"I'm empty of them now," she said. "What will you do when they leave?"

"Run a ranch. It's always neglected during these programs. There will be a lot of government paperwork to catch up on, a lot of purchases for the rest of the year, preparation of brochures for cattle sales. There's plenty to keep me occupied."

"And what will you do for pleasure?"

"Pleasure?" he asked. "What's that?"

"What I just saw tonight. You had some happy kids

and staff, too. And you're helping some mustangs find a home."

He smiled. "I guess you're right," he said. "I really would like to add a second program but I can't do it while school's in session, and I don't want to enlarge the one we have. Four seems to be the optimal number. More than that, and one or two kids will get lost.

"The first session," he admitted wryly, "didn't go as well as this one. I followed another model but it was stringent. The kids never relaxed. If they don't relax, the horse doesn't relax. It's a vicious cycle. It's the buddy system that makes this one work."

They were at the house. "Come in and have a glass of wine or something stronger," Reese invited as he held the door open.

"In the room that has no doors?"

"I have a study for friends. Sally has a sitting room for friends. That gives us both some privacy. The living room, dining room and kitchen are common use. In any case, I don't think there will be any roaming tonight," he said. "Chet's gone home. Sally and I have an agreement. We don't go in each other's wing if not invited. It's the only way it works. Chet's the only one that feels free to wander about."

"I like him."

"Everyone likes him, even when he fires them. That's a big plus in a ranch. Good ranch hands are hard to find and when you do, you want to keep them."

They were still at the door. She turned. "I think I would like that glass of wine."

He smiled. "Good."

"I'll go up and check on Julie first."

Jenny was in bed. Julie was in her pajamas. She wasn't

wearing the brace. "Look," she said as she crossed the room. There was a limp but the foot held steady.

"That's terrific. Why didn't you tell me it was so much better?"

"I wanted it to be a surprise. I think I still need to wear the brace while riding, though."

"It *is* a surprise, a wonderful surprise. Have a good time tonight?" Lauren said,

"It was great. So beautiful. I was happy that Jenny won, but we're all going to help with the menu. And I was so surprised by Heath. I didn't know he could sing like that."

Lauren hugged her, and her heart sang. Her daughter was a different girl than a month ago. "I have to go," she said.

"G'night," her daughter said sleepily.

Lauren went by her room and checked herself in the mirror. She ran a comb through her hair and glossed her lips. "Do you really want to do this?" she asked her reflection. Did she want to risk falling in love again?

It wasn't actually a date, she told herself. They were friends. *It's just a quick drink after a nice evening.* Yet she couldn't quite tamp the expectation. She pushed aside her reservations and went downstairs.

He met her in the living room. He'd changed into a fresh pair of jeans and a light blue sweater. It softened some of the hard angles of his face. He took her hand. "Let me show you my lair."

"Is that what it is?"

"Not until now."

"I've never been in a lair before."

"Then it's certainly time."

"I have to tell you my news first. Julie walked for me

just now. Without the brace or the crutches. It was better than I expected. Her foot will always be stabilized to a certain extent but she took some steps almost normally. She's going to have to be careful, though."

His fingers squeezed hers.

"That is terrific," he said, "and a cause for celebration." He opened the door to a large room decorated in beiges and rich dark browns. A desk was framed by a large window. A bar was built into one wall with a small fridge and wine cooler. The only other furniture was a large sofa, a coffee table and two large chairs. A large television was attached to the wall.

"This is my getaway place," he said. "My bedroom is down the hall. I do some of my work here."

It was decidedly masculine. There were two large paintings, one behind the bar and the other in back of the sofa. Both portrayed galloping horses, both in the same style. In one, the horses were splashing through a mountain stream. In the other, they were galloping through a mountain pass. In both they looked wild and free.

"Same artist?"

"Yep. A friend. Like me, a throwback. Sometimes I think we were born in the wrong century."

"You seem to be handling this one well," she observed.

He poured wine into two glasses and put them on a coffee table in front of the sofa, then guided her down on the sofa next to him. He put an arm around her.

"You feel good here," he said.

She snuggled into his arms. "You, too." She lowered her head against his shoulder.

He leaned down and kissed her, long and hard and soft and sexy and every other way he could conceive.

"I'm falling in love with you," he said as they came up for air.

She was startled. "I thought you weren't going to do that again."

"I'm having second thoughts. I don't want to lose you." His arms tightened about her. "I didn't think I could feel this way. I convinced myself that no woman could be happy here.

"But you," he continued, "don't only embrace challenges, you love them," he said. "I have a proposition. I really do need a business manager. Sandra wants to be with her mother more often and she and her husband also want to do some traveling.

"You can join us here in that capacity. I'll pay you the same as I paid her. You can have a cottage on the property and see if you and Julie like living here. See if it's a good fit. No pressure. I'm not sure I can make you happy. Winters can be hard here. They're beautiful but they can be lonely.

"I know you love flying," he said after a moment's silence. "I know you miss it."

"I do," she said, then added thoughtfully, "You know, there's a flying school and air service between here and Covenant Falls. Would the job of business manager preclude a part-time gig with it?"

"I know the school. Otis Davies. He's brought supplies for me when the roads are bad."

"He's offered me a job. Flying lessons. I told him I wouldn't fly in dangerous weather. Just lessons to keep my foot in the door."

He grinned. "I like it. I know what it means to love what you're doing. We can take it slow," he said. "What do you think? You can become my business manager while we see if it works for you," he said.

"What about Sandra?"

"She and her husband want to do more traveling. They don't need the income and I suspect she's been doing it as a favor to me."

"I don't know anything about ranching."

"If there's one thing I know about you, it's you're a fast learner and you're good with the monster—oops, I mean Maggie. Sandra will be available anytime you need her."

"How do you know I'm qualified? I've only made fake money on your computer."

"Well, it doesn't do that for me," Reese pointed out.

"How would your sister feel about it?"

"She mentioned once or twice that she wished you would stay."

"But to live on the ranch?" Lauren asked.

"Even happier. She's been trying to foist me off on someone for years."

"You told me you weren't going to get married again."

"That was a dumb statement. I'll never say never again."

"What about Julie?"

"I think she likes me. She loves Snowflake and Leo and she even likes Mistake," he argued. "She might be the only one."

"I know, but she was so close to Dane."

He held her closer. "We have a lot of time to figure it out."

The tough part was going to be telling Julie.

Ordinarily, Julie would be ecstatic to be in the midst

of so many animals, particularly Snowflake and Leo. But her daughter was also intuitive. And protective of her father's memory.

Lauren knocked on Julie's door at seven.

Julie opened it immediately. She was already dressed.

"Want to have breakfast with me this morning?" she asked. "We can take it outside to one of the picnic tables in back."

Julie immediately looked worried. "Is there a reason?"

"Well, yes. I want to talk to you about something."

"I'm not sure I like the sound of that," Julie said. "Did I do something wrong?"

"No. I think you'll like it."

Julie looked suspicious, then surrendered. She turned back to Jenny, who was going into the bathroom. "I'm having breakfast with my mom. Meet at the stables?"

"Okay. We all need to get together about the menu," Jenny called.

"Can't wait," Julie replied and joined Lauren in the hall. "What's up?"

"Let's get breakfast first."

"You're scaring me."

They went to the dining room and picked up plates, then went through the buffet. Julie chose all healthy foods, mainly fruit. Lauren needed courage. She chose bacon, a sweet roll and coffee.

"That will kill you, Mom, and you're the only parent I have," Julie said as they headed for the back of the house. It felt strange being scolded about health from her daughter.

Lauren waited until they were outside. No one else was there, except Leo, who followed them out the door.

"What is it?" Julie asked with panic and added, "You're not sick or something."

"No, it's good. Reese offered me a job here."

Julie stared at her. "What?"

"He wants to hire me as business manager. We would have a cottage here on the ranch."

Julie's eyes widened. "You're kidding me?"

"Nope. How would you feel about it?"

"Great. I mean living here! With the horses and Leo and Sally and Nathan." She paused, and Julie could almost hear her brain clicking away.

"Is there anything more to it?" Julie asked suddenly. "I mean, you and he are together a lot," she added with suspicion in her voice. "Everyone's noticed it."

"I like him as a person," she admitted, "but he had a bad marriage and I don't think he's ready to repeat it." She realized her mistake the moment the words came out.

"You *are* thinking about it. How can you even consider it? Dad hasn't been gone long, and you're thinking about someone else. Are you sleeping with him?" she asked furiously.

"No!"

"I don't believe you." Julie said. "I want to go back to San Antonio. My friends are there."

"You have friends here. We—you—*are* staying to the end of the program."

"I can't believe you're doing this. Tony said his mother is getting remarried and it's awful. He doesn't matter any longer."

"No one has said anything about marriage, and you will always be the most important person in my life."

"If I was, you wouldn't...do this."

She wasn't going to directly lie to Julie. That would

destroy a relationship that had been improving. "This is a great job, and I need one."

"You have all of Daddy's insurance money. Maybe that's what Mr. Howard wants."

"You can't believe that!" Lauren said. "That money has been put in a trust for you. I can't touch it. And no, he hasn't asked me to marry him, and we have no plans to marry. We're just friends."

"Are you going to sleep with him? Or have you been?"

"Julie!"

Julie stood and walked as fast as she could with her leg, probably to Snowflake. Leo, with his usual good instincts, followed her. Lauren couldn't go after her. She feared it would just make things worse and make Julie's accusations public. But Lauren had never seen her daughter so angry. She should have known. Should have realized. *Sometimes the truth is best not told.*

Maybe she should give Julie time to reconsider her first reaction. But then Lauren had second thoughts. She'd never felt the full force of Julie's anger before and had no idea where it would lead her daughter. A direct attack on Reese? Or some self-destructive action that might hurt herself? It was the latter that filled her with fear. She would call Reese, explain the situation, then find Julie and try to talk to her.

Her euphoria from this morning had just erupted into disaster.

Chapter 14

Reese was in the office, working on the payroll, when she reached him by phone. "I'm terrified she'll do something rash," Lauren said after recounting her conversation with Julie. "I've rarely seen her so upset. I'm going after her now, but I thought you should know if you see her first.

"I'm going down to the stable now," she added.

"I think a better person is Sally," he said. "She's been working with your daughter's leg as well as an instructor. I think Julie trusts her. I'll call her and explain."

"I didn't say anything other than what we talked about, that I would be business manager and she and I would have a cottage on the property," Lauren explained. "At first, she was excited about living here, but then she leaped to conclusions about our relationship. I think the loss of her father hit all over again." She knew her voice had a note of panic in it.

"She was so happy last night that her leg was better and she could walk without the brace," Lauren continued. "I really thought she would be excited about living here."

"I'm so damn sorry," he said. "It was probably way too soon to even propose it. It just seemed so right at the time. The last thing I wanted to do was create problems between mother and daughter."

"I shouldn't have mentioned the possibility yet. I should have waited but I really thought she would love the idea of living on the ranch."

Lauren broke off the conversation so he could call Sally, then went to the kitchen. Sally was in there already on the phone with Reese. She hung up. "I'll go down to the stable. Julie's probably with Snowflake. Our kids get really attached to their horses while they're here and confide all kinds of secrets and hurts to them."

"Shouldn't I go with you?" Lauren asked anxiously.

"I don't think so," Sally said softly. "Not if she's as angry as you think. A friend is probably more likely to get her to talk." She hesitated, then added, "I'm a hundred percent behind Reese's offer." Then she was off to the stable, leaving Lauren in a panic.

Lauren stayed at the window as Sally disappeared into the stables. A few minutes later, her phone rang. "She's gone," Sally said, "and Snowflake with her. Heath was there and said she just threw a saddle on Snowflake without the blanket and galloped out."

"She's still learning to ride," Lauren said. "If she acted that quickly, she probably didn't check the cinch."

"That's what I'm afraid of. I called Reese just before you. He's on his way. One of the hands is saddling Max

for him and a horse for me, and another hand is round-
ing up other riders."

"I want to help search," Lauren said.

"And you may go in an entirely different direction
than Julie and get yourself lost," Sally said gently. "The
best thing you can do is stay at the stables and organize
things. You're really good at that. Keep track of where
our people are going. And call our county emergency services. Tell them we've lost one of our Junior Ranchers."

"All right," she said reluctantly.

"My horse is saddled, and Reese and other riders are
on the way. Any idea where she might go?"

"I don't know."

"Okay, don't worry. We'll find her." The phone
clicked off.

Lauren called emergency services and told them her
daughter, a Junior Rancher, had taken off on a horse and
may be in trouble. The responder said they were on the
way with an ambulance.

As Lauren headed for the stables, the yard was filling up with more ranch hands headed into the building. She saw Reese give them each an assignment, then
stride over to her.

He gave her a sheet of paper. "These are riders and the
trails or directions they're taking," he said. "I'm going
toward the Roost. As more join us, have them scan the
list and find an empty spot. Okay?"

She nodded, trying to keep tears at bay.

"We'll find her," he said as he mounted Max.

Her heart hammered. Being unable to do more to help
was an agony she'd known too well during the months
her daughter was in the hospital. Why hadn't she concentrated on Julie?

An ambulance roared up and Jeff Henley, Chet's assistant, went out to meet it. She went running toward it, as well.

Jeff turned to her. "They're asking for medical information."

"Has she been found?"

"No, ma'am," the paramedic said, "We're just being cautious. You're Mrs. MacInnes?"

She nodded.

"Can you give us information about your daughter? Blood type?"

She could barely answer. All the images of the first time she saw Julie in the hospital sixteen months ago flashed through her head.

She tried to remember everything. Blood type of course and all the injuries Julie had incurred.

Betty came out of the kitchen and sat with her, holding her hand. Lauren was barely aware of it. Tears blinded her eyes.

An hour went by. She knew because she was clutching her cell phone in her hand. Jeff's phone went off. He talked for a moment, then reported.

"They found Snowflake. Her saddle had slipped. She's acting peculiar, doesn't want to leave. Reese thinks Julie must be close. They're searching that area now. He's asking for a stretcher on the trail to the Roost."

Fifteen minutes later, Lauren's cell rang and she heard Reese's voice. "We found her. We're bringing her in on the stretcher. I don't think there's any major injuries."

Fifteen minutes later four men rolling a stretcher trotted toward the ambulance. Reese rode behind them on Max and leading Snowflake.

Lauren ran over to the stretcher and leaned down. Julie's face was scratched and there were bruises and cuts. She reached out and grabbed Lauren's hand. The brace wasn't on her leg, but the paramedics said she'd known how to fall to protect it when the saddle came loose.

They said she would probably be in pain for a few days but there didn't seem to be major injuries. She would be x-rayed, though, at the county hospital.

"I'm sorry, Mom. Snowflake wanted to go back to the barn. I…think she knew something was wrong. Then the saddle slipped and I tumbled into some bushes. She wouldn't leave. I told her to go home. But she wouldn't.

"Then I heard some horses and my name called. I tried to yell, but it didn't sound very loud. It was Snowflake who brought them to me."

"We're going to the hospital now for X-rays," the driver interrupted.

Jeff stepped up. "I'll drive you, ma'am."

Lauren and Julie stayed at the hospital overnight. The X-rays didn't show any broken bones but she had some nasty bruises and several deep cuts from broken branches.

Jeff, Chet, Betty and Sally all came by late that day. Betty brought some soup, of course. Sally brought some wildflowers. Chet brought some candy.

When they were alone, Lauren took Julie's hand. "Until you have a child," she said, "you will never know how terrified I was for you. Please don't ever do that again."

"I'm sorry. Really sorry. I don't even know why I did what I did. I could have injured Snowflake and killed myself. You never would have gotten over it."

"No, I wouldn't," Lauren said. "I haven't gotten over

Dane's death. I never will. He'll always be one of the best parts of my life and he's why I'm who I am today. Just as I hope he would feel the same way if I'd died and he'd lived.

"He loved you so much," she added. "He's probably up there in the sky wondering why you took so little care with your own life."

Julie bit her lip and tears appeared in her eyes.

"I love you with all my heart, Julie. It would have broken again if anything happened to you and I was, in some way, responsible." She paused. She knew what she wanted to say but the words came hard. "I'm falling in love with Reese, but I'm not going to rush into anything.

"What I feel for him doesn't dismiss or demean Dane. It honors him because he showed me what love meant and how important it is. He always told me that he would be in the cheering section if I married again. He would know then he did a good job."

Tears flowed down both their cheeks and they held hands.

"I'm so sorry, Mom. I was afraid his memories would disappear." Tears hovered in her eyes.

"They could never do that, baby. He's engraved in our hearts. Nothing will take those memories away."

"I really do like Reese. I knew he would find me." Julie swallowed hard. "And I would like to stay here."

"Will you tell him that?"

"I will."

"Well, he's outside with a friend."

Lauren went over and opened the door. Reese came in, holding a vase full of columbines, the state flower of Colorado.

Leo galloped in ahead, put his two feet up on the bed and licked her.

Reese took one look at the two of them smiling and he grinned, as well. "I think Leo is trying to tell you what we all feel at Eagles' Roost. 'Welcome to our Colorado ranch.'"

Chapter 15

Julie graduated two weeks later with the other three participants in the program. Lauren watched proudly as the students first showed off their skills. They cantered, trotted, jumped, then each left their riding horse and eagerly led their mustang around the ring.

They didn't ride them. The mustangs were too newly trained and a sudden noise might startle them. Instead, the kids led their new friend with no mishaps other than an affectionate nip on Heath.

Not only were their parents in attendance but half of the community was there, too. Lauren watched with them as Reese proudly presented certificates and a sculpted horse to each one.

They were invited to return anytime. After they left the ring, all the ranch hands who had worked with them gave them a cowboy hooray.

There were long, sad goodbyes as they left. Jenny was in tears. The boys wore proud grins. Julie hugged each one with promises to keep in touch through text messages and Facebook as one after the other left.

She was limping as she walked over to Lauren and Reese. "I'll miss them," she said.

"You'll make a lot of new friends at school and you'll keep in contact with the others," Reese promised as he pulled on her ponytail. "They're welcome here anytime." Leo barked his agreement.

Lauren had moved into the cottage previously occupied by Chet and his wife. The ranch had bought the couple a new home in the nearby community of Paw Ridge. His former cottage would be too small with the baby coming, but it was just right as a temporary home for Lauren, who was now officially the business manager. Julie would move in today.

It was getting dark when the last visitor left. Sally retired to her rooms; Betty went to spend some badly needed time with her husband. Julie went with Nathan to feed the mustangs. Mistake tailed behind, braying for attention.

"Want to go to the Roost?" Reese asked Lauren.

It had become their favorite place in the past few days. Julie had accepted their relationship after the talk in the hospital, had even seemed excited about staying at Eagles' Roost. She and Snowflake had bonded during that afternoon on the path.

And tomorrow Lauren would drive to Otis's air station. They had explored possibilities, and he had checked with the high school. There was, indeed, a demand now that his faculty was expanded to include a former air force fighter pilot. The interest was higher among girls. She would commute, driving there Friday morning and giving lessons Friday and Saturday. She would stay at the inn Friday night but drive back to Eagles' Roost Saturday afternoon.

She'd talked to Julie first. She'd told her about her first teacher and how he'd changed her life, and how safe it was. She didn't say that it was safer than a car.

Julie could even be the first pupil if she wished. To her surprise, her daughter had nodded. "I want to be like you," she said, and Lauren's heart swelled.

After Julie and Nathan went into the mustangs' stable, Lauren saddled Lady while Reese saddled Max.

It was a perfect evening. The sun was just reaching the mountains and the valley was flooded with nearly every shade of gold and scarlet and orange and red.

They rode silently to the Roost where the first Howard rested.

Then Reese dismounted and Lauren slipped down into his arms.

"Does this feel like home yet?" he asked.

"I think it did the day I arrived," she replied.

"And I think that's the day I fell in love with you."

"I was...perturbed."

"You were angry, and so damned pretty. I wanted to kiss you then."

"You can do so now."

He did, and it was long, and incredibly sexy, and they didn't want to let go of one another.

As frissons of heat ran through her, she wasn't sure she could wait a year for marriage. But she had promised her daughter when the subject was broached. Reese also wanted to wait. He wanted to be sure Lauren and Julie would be happy here, that the winter wouldn't dim their love.

She knew it wouldn't, but she understood.

Until then, they had this private part of the Roost. Now and, she knew, for their lifetime.

Epilogue

One year later:
The Paw County Truth Teller/Published since 1899

The wedding of the year recently took place in a columbine field near the Eagles' Roost Ranch.

A sea of cowboy hats mixed with air force uniform caps was noted by witnesses of the nuptials of Colorado rancher Reese Howard and former air force major Lauren MacInnes.

Mr. Howard is owner of Paw County's largest ranch, and the new Mrs. Howard is co-owner of the Davies/Howard Flight Academy.

The bride's daughter, Julie, was maid of honor, and the groom's nephew, Nathan Howard, was best man. They made a striking pair of young people. Mr. Howard's ring bearer was his dog, Leo.

The wedding was attended by all the ranch personnel at the Eagles' Roost Ranch, who came in trucks and on horses, and air force pilots who flew in on fixed wing aircraft. Also attending as special guests were past and present Junior Ranchers, graduates of the Eagles' Roost Junior Rancher program. The groups meshed well because they were all made of the same right stuff: risk-takers. Bold. Tough. Convivial.

Since all reportedly appreciate brevity, the official service was short but the festivities long.

The kiss was, well, censored.

It was also reported by anonymous sources that eagles were invited but declined, preferring their centuries-old home on the cliffs surrounding the ranch.

* * * * *

Editor's Note: A few local restaurants disagreed about the convivial description. However, the editor was present at the festivities and stands by his observation.

Editor's Note 2: We do know that hats and caps don't attend weddings on their own, but we liked the image.

Editor's Note 3: The *Truth Teller* sends its heartiest congratulations to the county's leading citizen and his new bride.

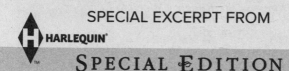

SPECIAL EXCERPT FROM

HARLEQUIN®

SPECIAL EDITION

*Alyssa Santangelo has no memory of the
past seven years—including her divorce—but she
remembers her love for Connor Bravo. One way
or another, she's going to get her husband back.*

Read on for a sneak preview of
A Husband She Couldn't Forget,
*the next book in Christine Rimmer's
The Bravos of Valentine Bay miniseries.*

An accident. I've been in an accident. The stitches they'd
put in her knee throbbed dully, her cheeks and forehead
burned and she had a mild headache. Every time she took
a breath, she remembered that the seat belt had not been
very nice to her.

She must have made a noise, because as she sagged
back to the pillow again, Dante flinched and opened
his eyes. "Hey, little sis." He'd always called her that,
even though she was second eldest, after him. "How you
feelin'?"

"Everything aches," she grumbled. "But I'll live."
Longing flooded her for the comfort of her husband's
strong arms. She needed him near. He would soothe all
her pains and ease her weird, formless fears. "Where's
Connor gotten off to?"

Dante's mouth fell half-open, as though in bafflement at her question. "Connor?"

He looked so befuddled, she couldn't help chuckling a little, even though laughing made her chest and ribs hurt. "Yeah. Connor. You know, that guy I married nine years ago—my husband, your brother-in-law?"

Dante sat up. He also continued to gape at her like she was a few screwdrivers short of a full tool kit. "Uh, what's going on? You think you're funny?"

"Funny? Because I want my husband?" She bounced back up to a sitting position. "What exactly is happening here? I mean it, Dante. Be straight with me. Where's Connor?"

Don't miss
A Husband She Couldn't Forget
by Christine Rimmer,
available October 2019 wherever
Harlequin® Special Edition books and ebooks are sold.

www.Harlequin.com

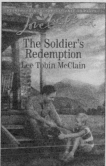

Looking for inspiration in tales
of hope, faith and heartfelt romance?

Check out **Love Inspired**® and
Love Inspired® **Suspense** books!

New books available every month!

CONNECT WITH US AT:

Facebook.com/groups/HarlequinConnection

Facebook.com/HarlequinBooks

Twitter.com/HarlequinBooks

Instagram.com/HarlequinBooks

Pinterest.com/HarlequinBooks

ReaderService.com

*Could a pretend Christmastime courtship
lead to a forever match?*

Read on for a sneak preview of
Her Amish Holiday Suitor, *part of Carrie Lighte's*
Amish Country Courtships *miniseries.*

Nick took his seat next to her and picked up the reins, but before moving onward, he said, "I don't understand it, Lucy. Why is my caring about you such an awful thing?" His voice was quivering and Lucy felt a pang of guilt. She knew she was overreacting. Rather, she was reacting to a heartache that had plagued her for years, not one Nick had caused that evening.

"I don't expect you to understand," she said, wiping her rough woolen mitten across her cheeks.

"But I want to. Can't you explain it to me?"

Nick's voice was so forlorn Lucy let her defenses drop. "I've always been treated like this, my entire life. *Lucy's too weak, too fragile, too small, she can't go outside or run around or have any fun because she'll get sick. She'll stop breathing. She'll wind up in the hospital.* My whole life, Nick. And then the one little taste of utter abandon I ever experienced—charging through the dark with a frosty wind whisking against my face, feeling totally invigorated and alive… You want to take that away from me, too."

She was crying so hard her words were barely intelligible, but Nick didn't interrupt or attempt to quiet her. When she finally settled down and could speak normally again, she sniffed and asked, "May I use your handkerchief, please?"

"Sorry, I don't have one," Nick said. "But here, you can use my scarf. I don't mind."

The offer to use Nick's scarf to dry her eyes and blow her nose was so ridiculous and sweet all at once it caused Lucy to chuckle. "*Neh*, that's okay," she said, removing her mittens to dab her eyes with her bare fingers.

"I really am sorry," he repeated.

Lucy was embarrassed. "That's all right. I've stopped blubbering. I don't need a handkerchief after all."

"*Neh*, I mean I'm sorry I treated you in a way that made you feel…the way you feel. I didn't mean to. I was concerned. I care about you and I wouldn't want anything to happen to you. I especially wouldn't want to play a role in hurting you."

Lucy was overwhelmed by his words. No man had ever said anything like that to her before, even in friendship. "It's not your fault," she said. "And I do appreciate that you care. But I'm not as fragile as you think I am."

"Fragile? You? I don't think you're fragile at all, even if you are prone to pneumonia." Nick scoffed. "I think you're one of the most resilient women I've ever known."

Lucy was overwhelmed again. If this kept up, she was going to fall hard for Nick Burkholder. Maybe she already had.

Don't miss
Her Amish Holiday Suitor *by Carrie Lighte,*
available October 2019 wherever
Love Inspired® books and ebooks are sold.

www.LoveInspired.com

LIEXP0919